THE MYSTERY OF THE
FLYING EXPRESS

AS JOE APPROACHED HE COULD HEAR FAINT MUMBLING.

The Mystery of the Flying Express   *Frontispiece (Page 168)*

THE MYSTERY OF THE FLYING EXPRESS

By
FRANKLIN W. DIXON

ILLUSTRATED BY
PAUL LAUNE

NEW YORK
GROSSET & DUNLAP
PUBLISHERS

CONTENTS

CHAPTER   PAGE

     I. A MYSTERIOUS GUEST 1

    II. THE NEW DETECTIVE 7

   III. THE STRANGE PROFESSOR 17

   IV. A FAMILIAR FACE 27

    V. THE ODD CODE 34

   VI. THE DISGUISE 42

 VII. THE HIDDEN SAFE 50

VIII. THE *Flying Express* 60

  IX. A DISTURBING TELEGRAM 70

   X. JOE DISAPPEARS 79

  XI. FOOTPRINTS 89

 XII. THE CLUE IN THE ASHES 98

XIII. A DARING RESCUE 107

XIV. A FIGHT ON THE PLAINS 116

 XV. THE SECRET PLAN 123

XVI. MUFFLED VOICES 132

XVII. FOLLOWED! 140

XVIII. AN ACCIDENT 149

XIX. THE TRAIN WRECK 158

 XX. TRAILING THE SUSPECT 167

XXI. THE CARVED SYMBOL 176

▼

Contents

CHAPTER   PAGE

XXII. A Big Discovery 183

XXIII. A Narrow Escape 191

XXIV. The Spy Camp 201

XXV. Closing the Case 209

CHAPTER I

A MYSTERIOUS GUEST

"There's such a thing as being too ambitious," drawled chubby Chet Morton, leaning back in his chair in the Hardy living room. "You're always on the go solving mysteries," he added to his chums, Frank and Joe. "Why don't you come on a vacation with——"

Crash!

With a whoop of alarm the stout lad landed on the floor, his chair overturned on top of him.

"That's the third time you've done the same thing in a few minutes," Frank Hardy exclaimed. "Once more, and we'll be calling the ambulance."

"I'll say so," agreed his fair-haired younger brother. "Chet, you'd better wear a parachute if you insist on rocking backward."

The lad picked himself up and rubbed his hands ruefully. "Well," he asked, ignoring the taunt, "how about that vacation?"

Frank's tanned, clear-cut face bore a thoughtful look. "Chet, your vacation idea isn't half bad. Trouble is, I think Dad is going to let Joe and me help him on one of his cases. He will tell us tonight." The older Hardy boy's voice sank to an undertone. "It's a very important case, too. It's in connection with——"

Just then Joe pretended to be seized with a violent coughing spell. "There, I guess I'm better now," he gurgled finally. "Had some dust or something caught in my throat." He eyed his brother significantly.

Failing to notice the look, Frank began whispering again. "As I was saying, this case is going to be a humdinger. Dad says it's one of the riskiest he's ever tackled."

In speaking of his father, he referred to Fenton Hardy, the famous detective.

"Why is it so dangerous?" Chet queried, open-mouthed.

"Because some of the most notorious——"

Frank stopped abruptly as Joe, with an exclamation, jumped from his chair and rushed across the spacious room. With a flick of his hand the younger lad whipped aside a heavy drape in the doorway to the hall.

"Agh!" crackled a guttural voice.

To the boys' astonishment a heavy-set, scowling fellow in working clothes stood before them.

"What are you doing here?" Joe demanded.

The man clenched his fists for an instant, then

seemed to gain control of himself. An unpleasant smile crept over his thick lips.

"I? What—am I—doing here? I am waiting for the money which is—owing to me." He spoke slowly in measured tones.

"The money? What money? What are you talking about?" Joe was growing angrier by the second.

Frank stepped alongside his brother with set jaw, while Chet gaped at the scene from a far corner of the room.

"Young men, you—will gain nothing—by becoming excited," said the intruder quietly. "I am—a man who fixes locks. The woman of your house—called me to fix the lock—on your back door."

The Hardys looked at each other questioningly.

"I have fixed it," continued the man. "The woman went upstairs to fetch my money, ten, maybe fifteen minutes ago. She has not come back, so—I came into the house—to find someone who will pay me."

Frank eyed the stranger hesitantly. "How much is it?"

"Oh, very little. Twenty-five cents," shrugged the other.

Thrusting his hand into a pocket, Frank withdrew a coin. "Here you are."

The man muttered a word of thanks, focussed his beady eyes on the boys for an instant, then turned and went out the front door. The chums watched him as he vanished beyond the hedge row. Then Joe wheeled around.

"There's something fishy about him, Frank."

Just then an elderly woman with a worried frown on her face hurried downstairs. "Frank! Joe! What's going on? Didn't I hear strange voices?" She peered around anxiously.

"Just one strange voice, Aunt Gertrude," Joe grinned. "By the way, did you or Mother order somebody to fix the lock on the back door?"

The boys' portly maiden relative paled. "I knew it, oh, I knew it," she moaned. "Burglars have broken in. I can see it in your faces."

"Now, Aunt Gertrude, please," Frank chided the woman impatiently. "Joe merely asked you a simple question. Nobody said anything about burglars."

"Hmph. Well, neither your mother nor I ordered any locks to be repaired, as far as I know. But I've been out all afternoon. Haven't seen your mother. M-i-l-d-r-e-d!" Her shrill voice resounded throughout the house.

A moment later the boys' mother, a slender, graceful woman, came down the stairs. "What is it, Gertrude? Has something gone wrong?"

Frank explained the incident. Mrs. Hardy shook her head. "It's a mystery to me, boys. There is nothing wrong with the back door lock so far as I know. I was out and came back just ahead of Gertrude."

"Then no one was here all afternoon," said Frank, for the three boys had been in the house only a short while.

"Maybe the fellow was trying to change the lock and come back later to rob you," suggested Chet.

"Wait a minute," Joe interrupted.

He felt in his trouser pockets and brought out a case of keys. Selecting one, he inserted it into the back door lock. There was a ready click.

"This hasn't been touched," he exclaimed. "It makes the same sound it always did."

Frank whistled in surprise. Then he scowled. "What a sap I was to pay that fellow and let him get away," he groaned. "Say, maybe we'd better have a close look around the house. Aunt Gertrude may be right. Perhaps he already has robbed us."

Ten minutes later Frank joined his brother and Chet in the living room. "There's certainly nothing missing," the older Hardy lad declared after a search. "What do you suppose that fellow really wanted?"

Joe pursed his lips. "I can't imagine, but I think we better check up on all the locksmith and hardware shops. Maybe we can find out where he works."

With Chet puffing along behind them the boys made a quick round of Bayport, not omitting the poorer stores skirting the edge of Barmet Bay on the east side of town. Their efforts to find an employee fitting the stranger's description were in vain. At length, as mystified as ever, they returned to the Hardy home on Elm Street and flopped into chairs.

"There goes our vacation," Chet grumbled. "I can see right now that we're at the beginning of another mysterious case of some sort."

"Maybe so, and then again maybe not," Frank remarked absently. "At any rate, I think I have an idea."

"So have I," Joe said, "and I think we'd better carry it out pronto. We'll change all the locks in the house. That fellow probably has had keys made for them by now. That's what he was doing, getting impressions of the locks."

Chet jumped up as if he had been shot. "Say, I'll bet that's just what he was up to. Jumping crickets, a fellow isn't safe anywhere these days. Now I *know* we'd better go on a vacation." The stout lad began pacing up and down the room worriedly.

Suddenly Frank seized his brother's arm. "Listen, Joe. If our friend the locksmith *has* been up to something like that let's go him one better."

The boys drew their chairs close together as Frank began whispering excitedly.

CHAPTER II

THE NEW DETECTIVE

Joe shook his head vigorously. "Run electric wires into the keyholes? Shucks, Frank, we don't want to give the fellow a shock. That would scare him away before we could catch him. No, that's out."

For several moments the boys were silent, thinking. Suddenly Frank uttered a low exclamation.

"I have it, Joe. We'll wire the locks, all right, but we'll run the wires to some sort of a signal inside the house. Then whoever's trying to get in won't know we've been warned."

"That's a good idea, Frank. What sort of signal shall we use? How about rigging up the radio so it'll turn on if someone puts a key in one of the locks? Nobody'd ever suspect the radio as a signal."

Chet yawned. "You fellows are going to have some job fixing keyholes so they'll turn on radios. Besides, it's just about suppertime and I'm hungry enough to eat a horse. See you two later."

With several grunts and a long stretch the plump lad pulled himself from the sofa and waddled out the front doorway.

"So long, Chet," Joe called, glancing at his watch. "By golly, it's time for Dad."

"Good evening, fellow detectives," boomed a hearty voice just then.

The boys looked up to see a tall, handsome man framed in the doorway, smiling at them.

"Hello, Dad!" Frank and Joe exclaimed together.

"Hello, boys. Do I observe signs of a recent conference of great importance? If my surmise is correct, I should warn you against getting Chet Morton upset!" There was a merry twinkle in his keen gray eyes.

Joe looked at his father admiringly. "Well, Dad, you win again. Maybe Frank can figure out how you knew we were having a conference and that Chet was in a dither, but I can't."

"I give up, Dad," his brother decided.

Fenton Hardy smiled broadly. "Nothing could be simpler than my deductions, boys. There are your chairs, two of them, drawn up near the sofa. From the depth of the depression in it I am quite certain our friend Chet has been lying there. Obviously you boys have been sitting in the chairs, and from their position you have been talking something over."

"Right you are, Dad," Joe cried out in delight. "But how did you know that Chet was worrying?"

"Simple enough. You will see that the nap of the carpet has been flattened in a broad track alongside the sofa. From the position of the track it must have been made by the person who was lying on the sofa. Since the nap of a carpet does not remain flattened for very long the track must have been made within the past half hour."

Mr. Hardy paused as the boys' smiles of delight grew broader.

"So," the detective continued, "putting our facts together, we may be reasonably certain that something you said disturbed Chet, and he got up and began pacing the floor alongside the sofa."

Joe made a wry face. "Shucks, Frank, we'll never be detectives. I couldn't have figured all that out."

"Neither could I," his brother admitted sheepishly. Then his face clouded. "Joe, we'd better tell Dad about that locksmith."

The sons related the incident in detail, while their father listened attentively.

"You say you have a plan?" the detective inquired.

"We thought we'd wire the locks, Dad, and hitch them up so the radio will turn on if anybody puts a key in one of them," replied Frank.

Fenton Hardy nodded approvingly. "Very good. How long will it take you?"

"I think we can finish the job before dinner. Come on, Joe, let's get busy."

The boys made half a dozen trips to their cellar tool shop and worked industriously for the next three quarters of an hour. At length, just as the dinner gong sounded, Frank gave a suppressed whoop of delight.

"There we are, Joe. Everything's ready. Here, try a key and let's be sure the idea works."

Joe slipped a key into the front door lock. Excitedly the boys listened.

"This is Station WMC," boomed a sonorous voice from the living room. "It is now one minute after seven o'clock . . ."

"That's great, Frank," the younger Hardy lad exclaimed. "I'll shut it off and we'll eat."

The boys could scarcely contain themselves during the meal, though both had misgivings about whether or not their visitor of the afternoon would attempt to return. Dessert finished, they lost no time in retreating to their father's study, where Fenton Hardy joined them.

"Now, boys, don't get your hopes too high," the detective warned gently. "Your friend the locksmith may not be in such a hurry to come back. Anyhow, while we're waiting, I have some things to talk over with you."

This was by no means the first conference Fenton Hardy had had with his two sons. An internationally known detective, formerly associated with the New York City Police Department but now operating privately, Mr. Hardy long had looked forward to the day when Frank and Joe would follow in his footsteps.

To his delight and somewhat to his wife's

alarm the boys had been keenly interested in their father's work from the time they were first able to understand it. Now, although they were still school boys, Frank and Joe had helped their father in solving mysteries and running dangerous criminals to the ground. The boys, indeed, had built up reputations of their own, and in Bayport and the surrounding countryside they were considered geniuses in the matter of crime detection.

Their first success had occurred when they located some valuable loot which a dying criminal confessed to them had been hidden in a tower. On another occasion Frank and Joe had become involved in a series of desperate undersea exploits. The far-famed adventure of "The Disappearing Floor" added another startling chapter to their exciting lives, while their weird experiences in the solution of the mystery of "The Twisted Claw" gave their reputations even further emphasis.

At the present moment, however, neither Frank nor Joe was thinking of the past. In solemn, hushed tones their father was outlining the part they were to play in a certain mission. It gave promise of being the most dangerous they ever had attempted.

"The Federal Government will stand behind us in this task, boys," Fenton Hardy was saying. "Our goal is to track down certain sinister spies who at present are endeavoring to destroy our whole social order. These spies are desperate men and I shall need all the help you lads can give me.''

''You can count on us to do anything you say, Dad,'' Joe promised fervently, and Frank nodded an emphatic agreement.

''I'm sure of that, boys.'' The detective paused for several moments. ''Well,'' he began again, ''here is the story.'' His voice dropped even lower. ''It seems that the Federal Government has evidence to the effect that there is a training school for spies right here in our own country.''

''Whew!'' Joe whistled. ''Can you imagine that?''

''The nerve of them,'' Frank exclaimed. ''Where is this training school?''

''That's just the point, Frank, nobody knows where the place is,'' the detective said grimly. ''From what evidence we have, however, we believe it to be located somewhere in the West.'' He looked at his sons earnestly. ''Boys, I want you to find it.''

A long moment of silence followed, broken only by the ticking of a grandfather clock. Frank looked at his brother.

''Well, Joe, do you think we'll be able to locate the place?''

''Just give me a tenth of a chance,'' Joe responded enthusiastically. ''Think of those fellows, Frank! Training men right here in our own country to upset our government.''

Frank clenched his fists. "Dad, if that institution is anywhere between the Atlantic and Pacific Oceans we'll get to it! We'll——"

"Our next selection will be *Stars and Stripes Forever* by Philip Sousa," interrupted a loud voice from the living room.

"The radio!" exclaimed Joe, leaping to his feet.

"Sh," Fenton Hardy warned. "Joe, take the back door. Frank, you take the front. I'll have a look at the side."

Through the gloom of the living room, where they had purposely dimmed the lights, the boys and their father hurried like flitting ghosts. Reaching the massive oaken front door Frank stopped and cocked an ear. His heart skipped a beat as he heard the unmistakable grating of a key in the lock.

Drawing a quick breath the lad flung open the door and charged headlong at a dim, heavy-set figure on the porch. With a dull *smack* Frank collided with it and his victim went crashing to the floor.

"I'll teach you——" the Hardy boy ground out fiercely, rolling over directly on top of the other. A split second later his fingers found the heavy-set intruder's windpipe.

"*Glug!* H-h-hey—l-lemme go!" gasped a voice.

With a chill of alarm Frank peered through the darkness at the face. "Chet Morton!" he yelped. "For goodness' sake!" Quickly he pulled his chum to his feet and searched for bruises.

"I—I guess I'm all right," spluttered the fat boy. "Jumping hoptoads, though, I'd hate to have you really mad at me. Jiminy, what a grip you had on my throat." Chet's eyes rolled and he made a grimace.

"Golly, I'm sorry as anybody could be, Chet," Frank apologized sincerely. "I forgot you had a key to the house."

"You gave it to me when I was here taking care of your Aunt Gertrude," Chet drawled, regaining his composure rapidly. "You really wired up those locks, didn't you? I thought you fellows were just kidding about that."

"Kidding nothing! But say, Chet, what'd you use your key for? You usually ring the bell."

The fat boy heaved a mighty sigh. "I was coming to that, Frank, if I hadn't been so rudely interrupted." He grinned. "But I really think I ought to tell your father about what I saw."

The Hardy boy eyed his chum in surprise. "You saw something, Chet? Come on in. We'll tell Dad right away."

Just then two figures hurried around the side of the house toward them. Frank recognized his father and Joe.

"Hello, what's up?" the latter called out in a hoarse whisper.

"I caught our man, all right, but he is the

wrong one," Frank laughed sheepishly. "But Chet says he has something to tell us."

"Better come inside," Fenton Hardy suggested. "The night air may have ears."

In the living room Chet settled himself into the softest chair with a sigh of relief. "Well, Mr. Hardy, I don't know whether this is important or not," the stout lad said in a whisper, "but when I heard you talking so loudly, just when I was coming up the front walk——"

"Talking loudly?" Fenton Hardy raised his eyebrows, while the boys looked at their chum in surprise.

"Golly, Mr. Hardy, I could hear you a block away, nearly. Anyhow, just as I was coming up the steps I saw somebody in the bushes next to the porch."

"You did?" Frank and Joe muttered together.

"I figured that fellow, whoever he was, was listening to Mr. Hardy tell all about his secret plans," Chet went on. "I decided the faster I got inside the house to warn you the better. I decided to act as if I hadn't noticed that fellow in the bushes, then let myself in with the key and warn you before that spy knew what was going on. Then, well, you know what happened next."

As the stout lad settled himself with a grunt, the Hardys gazed at one another dumbfounded.

"You weren't talking very loudly, Dad,"

Frank murmured in astonishment. "Chet, are you sure it was *Dad's* voice you heard?"

The fat lad nodded vigorously. "I ought to know Mr. Hardy's voice by now. I can even tell you everything he said."

"What do you make of it?" Joe pressed eagerly in an undertone.

"I think I have the answer, boys," Fenton Hardy whispered mysteriously. "Can you guess?"

CHAPTER III

THE STRANGE PROFESSOR

"WELL," said Mr. Hardy when none of the boys ventured an explanation of his supposed loud talking, "a good detective always reasons things logically. Now, can't you lads figure how Chet heard me outside?"

Joe grinned sheepishly. "A dictaphone, of course. Why didn't I think of that right away? That's the only possible answer."

"Exactly," his father agreed with a smile. Immediately his face clouded. "But that means something serious afoot, boys."

"I'll say it does," Frank muttered. "And what's more, now we know what that locksmith was doing this afternoon. He was wiring the house for the dictaphone."

Jumping up from his chair Joe grabbed his brother's arm. "Come on, let's find those wires and get rid of them, Frank."

The boys started their search outside the house, first making a hasty inspection of the premises to make certain no one was about. Then, with the aid of flashlights, they examined the walls of the house minutely. Suddenly Joe uttered a soft cry.

"Come here, Frank!"

His brother hurried to where Joe knelt among some shrubs planted near the house.

"By golly, that's it, all right. Look, there's the amplifier. Where does it go to? There's the wire!"

"Runs right into the cellar window. We'll be able to trace it from inside easily enough."

Clipping off the amplifier instrument Frank stuffed it inside a pocket and the two boys hurried into the cellar.

"There's the wire coming in, Joe. Look, it goes up through that hole in the boards."

"Right into Dad's study, Frank."

Hurrying upstairs to their father's den they soon picked up the wire again, and a moment later located a tiny microphone hidden near a radiator.

"Careful how you touch it, Joe. We'll want to examine the fingerprints on it first."

"Right. I'll carry it down to the laboratory in a handkerchief. All set?"

"Yes. I'll bring some of the wire too. Probably plenty of marks on it."

Returning to the cellar where the boys had a well-equipped fingerprint laboratory, Frank and Joe spread out their paraphernalia and promptly went to work.

"We'll take microphotos of the prints and take them down to Police Headquarters first thing in the morning," the older lad decided.

"Right, Frank. We ought to know who the fellow is by lunch time. Then there'll just be the matter of catching him."

"Yes, that's all," Frank grinned. "Here's the first print. Ready with the camera?"

Faint whorls had appeared on the microphone, beneath the special powder Frank had been spraying over the instrument. Quickly Joe focussed his combination camera and microscope, while Frank prepared the developing fluid.

Half an hour later, perspiring but happy, the boys emerged from the basement with a sheaf of photographic prints portraying in greatly enlarged size a series of fingerprints. Their father nodded approvingly when he saw them.

"Excellent work, boys. Chief Finch at the Bayport Station will be glad to go over his files with you tomorrow, I know."

Frank and Joe lost no time making for the Bayport Police Headquarters immediately after breakfast the following morning. They were ushered at once into Chief Finch's office.

"Hm," said the fat, genial officer. "Fine prints, these. Oh, Barclay. Have these checked right away."

A uniformed guard attended to the errand, while the boys chatted with Chief Finch, whom they had known for years. At length the second officer returned, shaking his head.

"Nothing on the records like these, Chief,"

he said. "I sent 'em by telephoto to New York to see if they had anything to compare with 'em and they wired back 'No.' "

Greatly disappointed, the brothers thanked Chief Finch, who promised to do his best to help them, and went out onto Main Street.

"Now what?" Joe wondered.

"Looks as if we're stuck. Still, there's one thing we can do. We can search all the stores in town."

"There's nothing to lose if we do, Frank. That fellow might be working in most any kind of a shop."

Commencing at the west end of Main Street the boys, on various pretexts, went into each and every store on both sides of the block. Lunch time found them wearily standing in front of a high-class restaurant, their task not more than a third finished.

"Well, I'm for knocking off for a bite to eat, Frank. What say?"

"Suits me. Say, look here." His brother pointed to a large sign in the restaurant window.

"Professor Transor Reads Character and Identifies Residence Locality of Customers By Their Speech," Joe read aloud. "Hmph. Wonder what kind of a man he is."

"I've a hunch it might be interesting to find out," Frank said, his face brightening. "At least we can get something to eat at the same time."

The restaurant was not crowded and the boys had a clear view, from where they sat, of the supposed professor at a small table at the far end of the room.

"He's pretty young," Joe whispered. "Looks more like a handsome movie star than a professor."

"He certainly doesn't look like a fake, anyhow. Seems like a nice fellow."

A waiter stepped up to take their order. "How much is the professor's fee?" Frank queried.

"Two dollars for a reading, sir," replied the waiter. "The gentleman, he is very good. You will like him ver' much."

Frank gave their order for luncheon, then looked at his brother excitedly. "Joe, I just had an idea."

"What is it?"

For several moments the boys whispered together. When the waiter came back with their food they were grinning broadly.

"Will you reserve some time for us with the professor?" inquired Frank.

The boys ate their roast beef quickly and impatiently waited until the man finished with another client.

"The professor is now ready," said the waiter, motioning them to step forward.

The character reader's bright, eager eyes rapidly surveyed them. "How do you do, young men?" he greeted in a pleasant voice. "Which of you wishes the first interview?"

Frank nodded toward Joe.

"Very well," continued the man, fingering a wispy moustache. "First, before reading your character, I shall endeavor to tell you where you live merely by the way you speak."

Joe nodded with a smile.

"Now, you must know that language distinctions are quite marked, if one has studied them minutely," the professor explained. "Accents differ slightly in each state and often in towns close together. Of course if you are foreigners, the matter will be even simpler."

The speaker looked at Joe sharply as the brothers exchanged meaningful glances. The younger Hardy lad's face flushed slightly.

For a moment the professor watched them. Then, clearing his throat, he said, "Now then, young man, will you please begin speaking? Tell me something, anything. Why do you eat in restaurants?"

Joe was smiling broadly. "Agh!" he exclaimed suddenly, "this restaurant—is a good place. My brother and I are exceedingly fortunate—to be able—to afford such a—place."

The man slapped his hand on the table and leaned back in his chair. His penetrating gaze all but riveted Joe to the spot.

"Young fellow," he said haughtily, "your accent is not your own. You have deliberately assumed a false manner of speaking."

As Joe's face turned crimson, Frank spoke up.

"Please forgive us, Professor," he said earnestly. "We really had a serious purpose in mind, as I'll explain. In the meantime let me introduce us to you. I'm Frank Hardy and this is my brother Joe."

The professor's face relaxed somewhat. "Hardy? Are you by chance related to Fenton Hardy, the detective?"

He smiled broadly when Frank told him they were. "I am very glad to know you, boys," he said warmly. "You see, I, too, am interested in crime detection, for I am a psychologist at Bixby University. Psychology plays an important part in crime, as you know. I am working on a pet theory of mine and trying to interview as many people as possible. A restaurant is a good place to meet all kinds. But, tell me, were you just playing a joke on me a few moments ago?"

"We certainly were not," Frank replied. "We were just trying to trace a burglar by his speech."

"Your brother is a good mimic," the professor declared. "Still, his accent gave itself away as being artificial. There is no such accent naturally. The exclamation 'Agh!' was the only genuine part of your little speech, Joseph."

"The stranger we are looking for spoke to us just as Joe imitated him this very minute, Professor," the older Hardy lad said. "I thought that maybe you could give us some kind of a clue as to where you think the fellow might have come from.''

The psychologist, who said his name was Henry Transor, leaned back thoughtfully. ''Well,'' he observed at length, ''all I can tell you is that his accent was entirely faked, if it sounded like Joe's imitation.''

''Hm,'' said Frank. ''That certainly complicates matters all the more.''

''It is possible he is a foreigner,'' suggested Professor Transor. ''The precise, halting speech is a characteristic of aliens trying to lose their accents. Now, of course, my old teacher, Professor Clyde Morse——'' Transor hesitated and gazed off reflectively.

''Professor Morse!'' Joe exclaimed. ''I've heard of him. Wasn't he a famous——''

''Professor Morse was the greatest authority on languages the world has ever seen,'' said Transor proudly. ''He was my teacher at Bixby University. Professor Morse was the one man who could teach a person a different accent from his own so thoroughly that nobody ever would be able to tell that he hadn't spoken that way always.''

''I remember something about Professor Morse,'' Frank said meditatively. ''Wasn't he killed, or didn't something terrible happen to him? I forget just what.''

Transor looked away thoughtfully. ''No, Professor Morse wasn't killed, so far as anybody knows. But he disappeared. Never came back from his summer vacation one year. The worst of it is, he was at work deciphering an ancient manuscript which contained some chemical formulas.''

''What good would ancient chemical formulas be?'' Joe shrugged. ''Nobody wants them now.''

''On the contrary,'' contradicted the professor, ''these formulas seemed to be ahead of our times. They gave promise of astounding revelations.'' He lowered his voice and furtively looked around the room. Seeing no other customers within earshot he went on, ''The United States War Department was greatly interested in them!''

''Has the War Department put them to use?'' Frank queried.

''That's just the trouble, they can't. Professor Morse had deciphered enough of them to show their astonishing value, but not enough so they could be fully explained. The War Department experts have been unable to finish what Professor Morse started.''

An interval of tense silence followed as the boys pondered their friend's strange tale. Finally Joe spoke. ''Hasn't a clue to Professor Morse's disappearance ever been found?''

''None whatever,'' returned the other grimly. ''He vanished a few years ago. So far as I know he had no enemies, nor was he the kind of man who worries.''

Frank glanced at his watch. "Well, Joe, I suppose we ought to get started. It's after two o'clock."

Could the boys have witnessed their Aunt Gertrude's expression at that moment they would have been off for home like a shot with-out so much as a by-your-leave to the professor. The elderly woman was standing on the second-floor landing of the Hardy home with terror etched in every wrinkle of her face.

CHAPTER IV

A FAMILIAR FACE

"GOLLY, he's just about the most interesting fellow we've met in a long time, isn't he?" Joe exclaimed after the two boys had taken leave of Professor Transor and headed up Main Street.

"He certainly is. What I'd like to know more about is what happened to Professor Morse. Maybe some day we'll have a chance to work on that mystery."

"Oh, probably he is dead, Frank. You know, I have a hunch that we ought to go home and check up on things. Aunt Gertrude is there by herself today."

"That's right, Mother was to be out and Dad went to Pottsville in connection with his new case. Still, he put some new inside bolts on all the doors last night. He told Aunt Gertrude to keep them locked while we were out."

The brothers decided nevertheless that a brief visit home before continuing their search of Bayport's stores would be in order. Accordingly they turned their footsteps toward the west end of town and soon rounded the corner into Elm Street.

"Everything looks quiet enough from here,"

Joe observed casually as they approached the house.

"We'll have to ring the doorbell on account of the inside bolts. Won't Aunt Gertrude be mad if we wake her from her nap?" Frank grinned.

Mounting the front steps he pressed the button. There was no response.

"Give it another try," urged his brother. "Aunt Gertrude's a pretty sound sleeper."

Though they could hear the bell chiming deep inside the house, no response was forthcoming.

"That's funny," Frank murmured. "You don't suppose she's out at some—hello, what's this?"

The lad had given the door a slight push. To their surprise it swung open.

"A-u-n-t G-e-r-t-r-u-d-e!" Frank called.

The ticking of the grandfather clock was their only answer. Suddenly Joe touched his brother's arm.

"Frank! Listen!" Something that sounded like a low moan could be heard near by. "Look!"

The boy pointed to a woman's shoe protruding from beneath a heavy drape near the staircase. Instantly both boys sprang to the spot. Whipping aside the material they found their aunt sprawled on the floor.

"Get some water, Joe. It's just a faint, I think." Frank knelt and took the old lady's head in his arms. "Aunt Gertrude! Wake up!"

After a few applications of water the woman's eyelids began to flutter.

"Oh, dear," she groaned. "Oh, dear, something terrible—my goodness!" Her eyes flew wide open and she stared wildly at the boys. "Where am I?"

"You're all right, Auntie," said Frank soothingly. "We'll help you to the sofa."

Quakingly, with Frank's help, the woman tottered to the couch and sank down with a sigh.

"Air," she gasped. "Let me have air."

"There, there, Aunt Gertrude," Joe said. "Tell us what happened."

"Murderers," the woman gasped. "Murderers and robbers. I saw them!"

"Murderers and robbers? Where did you see them?" Frank asked tolerantly.

"Right there—in your father's study. Standing there looking at me when I came downstairs. Oh," shrieked the nervous old woman, "never shall I spend another night in this house. Never again——"

"Why didn't you have the inside bolts locked, Aunt Gertrude?" Frank asked.

"Oh, I know it was my fault. Everything is always my fault," she moaned.

"Please quiet yourself," Frank coaxed. "Otherwise we can't help you."

Gradually their relative regained such composure as she normally possessed. "Very well, I unlocked the inside bolts because I wanted to take a nap and I didn't want to have to let you boys in. Then I heard a queer noise downstairs. When I came down to see what it was, I saw those murderers and burglars."

"How many were there, Aunt Gertrude?" Joe queried, winking at his brother.

"There must have been half a dozen," whined the patient. "At least there were three or four."

"Did you actually *see* three or four?" Frank pressed, well aware of his relative's flair for exaggeration.

Aunt Gertrude hesitated, pouting. "Well, n-not exactly," she admitted. "But there was one horrible-looking man and I'm sure there must have been more in the——"

"There was one, anyhow," Joe grinned at Frank.

"Was he a heavy-set fellow, Auntie? With pudgy lips and shifty eyes?" the older Hardy lad asked.

The woman frowned reflectively. "I—I think he was. Yes, I'm certain of it. And he had on some filthy workman's clothing. Oh!" She shuddered and drank some of the water Joe offered her. "Now, boys, I don't want to hear any more about it."

Frank motioned to Joe and the two boys retired into their father's study.

"Same fellow?" Joe raised his eyebrows.

"Must be, if Aunt Gertrude's description is to be relied upon. It's our locksmith, sure as shooting."

"We'd better not say too much, then. Can't ever tell, he may have the house wired with dicta-phones again," decided Frank.

"You're right," agreed Joe.

Frank went to his father's desk and found a piece of blank paper upon which he wrote some-thing hurriedly. He handed it to Joe, who read the following:

"Our locksmith friend is probably after some of Dad's important private papers. He's not prowling around just to hear our conversations over a dictaphone. We'd better have a look inside the private safe and see if everything's all right. You guard the entrance while I open the safe."

Joe looked at his brother and nodded. With-out a word Frank went upstairs with Joe close behind. They stopped before what appeared to be an ordinary closet door in one of the bed-rooms.

"I think Mother keeps the clean sheets in here, Frank," Joe said in a loud voice.

"I think she does. Wait, I'll have a look."

Frank opened the door, revealing a small closet with shelves loaded with bed linen. Deftly the boy cleared the third section of its burden. Then, with a quick look back at Joe, he reached to the wall behind the shelf and clicked open a small panel.

"I can't find that blue washcloth, Joe," he called over his shoulder. "Have you your flash-light?"

His brother handed one over. Then followed a series of dull clicks as Frank twirled a small knob gleaming in the rays of the beam. There was a loud snap, followed by a rustling of papers. More clicks sounded, then the boy drew out his head from the aperture, replaced the stacks of muslin, and came into the room.

"The blue washcloth's there, Joe, and I guess we have enough sheets and pillow cases to last for a while," he remarked casually. "Come on, let's go outside and get some fresh air."

Safe from prowling eyes and ears on the wide grounds surrounding their home Frank and Joe flopped on the ground for a conference.

"Dad's private papers were all intact, so far as I could tell," the older Hardy lad informed his brother. "Still, I think we'd better continue our hunt in the local shops, then get in touch with Dad to let him know what's been going on."

"Good idea," Joe agreed. "We'd better not take the chance of phoning from the house, though. Let's send him a wire from the railroad station."

Several hours of weary hunting brought no results in locating the mysterious locksmith. Discouraged, they went at dusk to the Bayport station where Frank sent off a telegram to Mr. Hardy at his hotel in Pottsville. Rejoining his brother a few minutes later, he noticed an expression of excitement on Joe's face.

"I was looking up trains for the West, Frank,

in case we should want to take one some day soon. The *Flying Express* is due to pass through here in five minutes. Goes this way every day. It's one of the best and fastest of all the trains heading for the Rockies.''

"Good. We'll probably be on it before the week's over. Let's watch her go through."

A mournful whistle sounded in the distance.

"Look, Frank," Joe suddenly whispered. "See that fellow going down the tracks?"

"Where'd he come from?"

"I just saw him step out of the bushes."

"There comes the flyer!" cried Frank. "Boy, look at her travel!"

Far down the track was the racing giant of the rails, coming at terrific speed.

"I'll bet that fellow is going to jump in front of the engine," added Frank nervously. "Look at him crouching there!"

"He looks familiar," Joe observed suddenly.

As the great express hurtled toward them, the Hardy boy uttered a cry and darted off toward the figure beside the tracks. Just before Joe reached the man, a large bundle was thrown from the observation platform of the rear car, landing with a thud alongside the rails. With a rush the man sprang forward and snatched the object.

Whirling about, Joe called frantically to Frank to lend his assistance, for the person with the package was the missing locksmith!

CHAPTER V

THE ODD CODE

"IT's our man, Frank!" Joe shouted.

Without waiting to see whether his brother understood, the younger lad dived headlong at the rough-looking stranger who had just received the bundle. The man was too quick for him. Before Joe could pick himself up, the other had disappeared through some bushes along the embankment.

Like a bolt of lightning Joe plunged after him. With the telltale quivering of leaves and small shrubs marking the man's trail, Joe soon caught sight of him ahead. With quickening pulse Joe saw that the fugitive was apparently making for a high trestle.

"Go back I—warn you!" yelled the man over his shoulder.

At the same instant he careened from the bushes, mounted the railroad track and began running. The river was a hundred feet below. Joe, just behind him, leaped over the ties three at a time.

"Go—back!" screamed the man again.

Instead of obeying, the boy gave a tremendous lunge with outstretched hands. With a yelp of triumph he caught the man's jacket in one fist, making a desperate attempt to yank him to a halt. The fugitive wrenched himself free with a twist that all but flung the youth from the trestle. Before the boy could regain his balance the stranger was out of sight.

"Joe! Are you all right?"

Jumping from tie to tie along the dangerous trestle Frank came hurrying toward his brother, anxiety on his face. Joe pulled himself to his feet with a wry grin.

"He got away, Frank. But he left something behind, and I'll bet it's important."

"What on earth are you talking about, Joe? Who is this fellow? I couldn't hear what you said when you called to me back there."

"He's the locksmith, Frank. I thought he looked familiar when we first saw him. When the train came along he looked right at me and I got a good view of him."

"Our locksmith, eh?" Frank pursed his lips. "Wish I'd come after you right away."

Joe pointed to the river below. "When I grabbed his coat he dropped that package. Someone on the observation platform of the flyer threw it to him. It's down there somewhere."

Frank looked at his brother. "How about getting out the *Sleuth* and looking for it?" he asked, referring to the boys' very fast motorboat.

Excitedly the boys hurried back over the trestle and took a short cut to town, where Frank hailed a taxi.

"The Yacht Club," he ordered as they jumped in.

The car roared off, arriving ten minutes later in front of a trim building on the waterfront. Frank paid their fare and they hurried along the pier to the *Sleuth*.

"I'll warm up the engine," said Frank.

There was a whining sound, then a throaty roar as the powerful motor sprang into life. In a few minutes the boat's prow was slicing through the rough water. Bayport gradually dwindled from view as they headed out into the broad bay, then turned into the mouth of Willow River.

"Better take soundings, Joe," Frank suggested, closing the throttle to quarter-speed. "Tide's running out and it looks pretty shallow around here."

Joe flung out the sounding line from his station at the bow and sang out the readings every few seconds. "Fifteen feet . . . fourteen . . . twelve . . . ten . . . seven . . . whoa, Frank, take it easy."

"There's the trestle up ahead."

"Seven feet . . . six and a half . . . Look out, Frank!"

There was a deep, grinding sound and the *Sleuth* shuddered to a sudden standstill. The brothers looked at each other in alarm.

"I think we'll wade up underneath the trestle, Joe. What's the reading here?"

Joe heaved over the line again. "A measly
three feet. It's probably only two underneath
the tracks."

"Good enough. Well, here goes."

Sitting down on the deck Frank pulled off
his shoes and socks and rolled up his trousers,
while his brother did likewise. Quickly the boys
slid overside.

"You'll have to lead this expedition, Joe.
You know where the package dropped."

"I think—let's see." Joe squinted overhead
at the lofty bridge and estimated the distance
he had run across it in the chase. "Over there,
Frank," he decided, pointing.

"Then let's start the diving," said his
brother. "Wish I had a helmet like the one we
used in the Secret Warning mystery."

"Guess we won't need helmets in two feet of
water," Joe laughed. "Hmph. What's this?"
Leaning down into the water the younger
Hardy lad tugged heavily at something. "Feels
like a bunch of paper."

An instant later he brought a large water-
soaked package to the surface.

"Newspapers," grunted Frank. "Is *that*
what you risked your life on a trestle for, Mr.
Detective?"

Joe frowned. "This certainly looks like the
bundle that fellow was carrying." He eyed
the soggy mass disgustedly.

"It hasn't been in the water very long," Frank observed. "Maybe we can read the papers if there's anything worth while in them."

"There must have been *some* reason why that fellow was so eager to get them," responded Joe.

"Let's take the package along, just for luck," his brother decided. "In the meantime I've a notion the water's getting deeper. We'd better get back to the *Sleuth* before she floats off without us!"

Frank started the engine, then opened the throttle to full speed astern. The craft quivered for an instant, then lunged backward into deep water. A moment later the boys were roaring toward the Yacht Club.

"Say, look here, Joe," called Frank, who had been gazing idly at the bundle as he piloted the boat. He pointed to the top of one of the newspapers.

"What do you see?"

"It's a western journal, Joe. Published in the town of Saddler. That's somewhere out near the Rockies, isn't it?"

"Never heard of it," Joe grunted. "Besides, I don't see what——"

"They're *all* from Saddler," went on Frank. "And look at those underlined words. What do you suppose they mean?"

To the boys' wonderment several of the sheets contained words that had been underscored by some sort of indelible pencil. Scrutinizing each of the newspapers in turn the boys discovered six underlined words in all. Frank jotted them down. Jones . . . faithful . . . East . . . Hunt . . . English . . . West.

"What do you make of that?" asked Frank.

"Just about as much as you do. In other words, nothing. Look out, you're going to hit that buoy!"

So absorbed had Frank been that he had all but forgotten the *Sleuth's* helm. With a flip of his wrist he pulled the wheel around, narrowly avoiding a large channel marker. For the next fifteen minutes they sped through the wide spaces of Barmet Bay and finally moored the *Sleuth* at the Yacht Club.

During their walk home the brothers spoke little. Each was absorbed in speculating on the possible meaning of the strange underlined words. At length they reached home with no solution in mind.

"Oh, it's you," their Aunt Gertrude exclaimed, unbolting the front door. "Thank goodness."

"Has Dad sent us any message, Auntie?" Frank inquired.

"No, he has not," the woman snapped. "Really, I should think your father would stay home once in a while. There's no telling what may happen around here." With that she stomped upstairs to her room and closed the door.

"Tell you what," said Frank. "Let's eat, go to bed early and then see if we can trace that locksmith's tracks first thing in the morning."

The sun had long since appeared over the horizon next day when Joe, still sleepy, heard a pounding on the front door.

"Hey!" came a muffled shout. "Are you all dead?"

The lad tumbled out of bed, slid downstairs, and opened the front door.

"Chet! For goodness' sake, what are *you* doing up?"

The fat boy smiled broadly. "What are *you* doing asleep?" he retorted. "I thought you two fellows never bothered to retire."

He followed Joe upstairs where Frank was slipping on his clothes. Seeing Chet, the older Hardy lad uttered an exclamation of astonishment.

"Never mind all the war whoops," Chet drawled humorously. "I'm really up and dressed, and I'll admit it's a bit unusual. But what about a picnic?"

Frank suddenly looked at Joe and winked. "A picnic, Chet? Say, that's not a bad idea. Want to start right away?"

"Sure, why not? The weather's fine. Let's take a boat ride somewhere."

Frank finished tying his necktie. "I think it would be more fun to take a hike, don't you, Joe?" He gave his brother a significant look.

"Sure thing, Frank. Why not go over to

Seaview Bluff? That's only about two hours' walk if we go along the railroad tracks.''

Chet made a grimace. ''What do you fellows always want to *walk* for? And anyhow who wants to walk along some old railroad tracks?''

''Aw, be a sport, Chet,'' Joe laughed, giving his plump chum a playful jab in the ribs. ''I know a wonderful place where we can eat at Seaview Bluff. Best hamburgers you ever tasted, really!''

The brothers took time for a hasty breakfast, then set out, with Chet waddling along between them. To the fat boy's surprise they marched straight for the railroad station, then toward the trestle.

''We're not going across *that* thing, I hope!'' Chet groaned, and it was only by dint of considerable persuasion that he could be induced to cross. Once they had reached the opposite end Joe stopped and began staring at the ground.

''What's the matter?'' Chet queried.

''There it is, Frank,'' said Joe in a suppressed voice. He pointed at a massive footprint clearly imprinted in the soft dirt near by.

''Yes, and there's another,'' Frank observed. ''They won't be hard to follow. Let's go.''

CHAPTER VI

THE DISGUISE

"Say, what's going on here, anyhow? I thought we were heading for a picnic," Chet pouted.

"We are," said Joe. "Come on, old boy, don't worry about a little thing like a few footprints."

"That's all right for you to say," the fat lad whined, "but I'm on to you fellows. First thing I know we'll be getting shot by gangsters. No siree, not for me!"

Frank nudged his brother. "It's only about half a mile to that restaurant we were talking about, Joe. Getting hungry?"

Chet's frown suddenly relaxed. "Say, I could stand a bite to eat. Only half a mile to those hamburgers?"

With Chet trudging along behind them in a better mood Frank and Joe swung over the narrow trail, pausing now and then to examine it. Soon, however, the boys found themselves confronted by the highway.

"Guess we'll have to hire a bloodhound if we want to pick up those marks now," Joe snickered.

"Hot diggety, there's the eating place," came a whoop from Chet. He indicated a rambling shack a few hundred feet down the road.

"That's it, all right," smiled Frank. "Well, I think I could manage to stuff away a hamburger or two. How about you, Joe?"

"Suits me," replied the latter with a wink.

A few moments later the three boys lined up along the counter of the establishment which a dingy sign proclaimed to be Mike's Munchery. Mike himself stood beaming before them.

"You be wanting something to eat, eh?" he grinned. "Hamburg', maybe?"

"Three of them, big ones," Frank grinned back.

"Make it two for me," Chet chimed in, eyeing the others sheepishly.

Chuckling to himself, Mike tossed the meat onto his grill with a practiced air. Soon a fragrant sizzle greeted the boys.

"Business good?" Frank inquired casually.

"Oh, not so good last few days," said Mike. "Half dozen people, maybe." He shrugged and flattened the ground steak with a large knife.

"Mostly tourists, I suppose," Frank commented.

"Oh, yes. Most' tourists. One fellow look like a workman. Nice fellow. Beeg!"

Mike threw out his chest to show them. Frank shot a quick glance at his brother. Could the patron have been the locksmith?

"Ya-as, very nice fellow," Mike rumbled on.

He tapped the grill with his knife. "He fixed this. My grill wouldn't work just when I needed it. This fellow, he fixed it fine!"

"That was good luck for you, wasn't it?" Frank remarked, to keep the man talking about his recent customer.

The proprietor flipped the cooked hamburgers onto rolls and set them down on the counter.

"The fellow had bad luck," said Mike. He disappeared into a back room and returned a moment later with a wrist watch. "He took this off when he work, and forget it. Maybe you know where he live, eh?"

Frank took the watch and examined it minutely, with Joe peering over his shoulder. After a moment the lad handed it back to Mike.

"Good watch. I don't know the fellow. He is certain to come back for it."

"When he does," Joe chimed in, "make him sign a receipt for it, Mike. That's the safest way to do."

"Yes?" blinked Mike. "Make him sign his name, eh?"

Joe nodded, exchanging a significant look with Frank. As Mike toddled into the back room with the watch Chet suddenly gave a mighty sigh.

"Boy, am I full! Golly, those were the best hamburgers I ever ate!"

The Hardys looked at each other, then at the food they had completely forgotten.

"Come on, Frank, we'd better catch up with

Chet before he orders another," Joe laughed.

The brothers downed their hamburgers so quickly that their fat chum winced. Then, waving good-bye to Mike, the boys filed out.

"Now what?" Chet wanted to know. "How about a nap under that tree?"

Frank frowned. "I hate to say it, Chet, but I think we'll have to call off the picnic. Joe and I have a little job ahead of us."

"I knew something like this would happen," the plump lad groaned. "Can't you fellows ever take a day off from your detecting?"

Frank laughed. "Why don't you stay with us? You can help."

Chet edged off. "No, thank you, fellows. I'm going home and find some peace and quiet. No work for me!" With a leisurely wave of his chubby hand he strolled off down the road.

"What are we going to do now, Frank?" Joe queried. "We can't trace those footsteps any farther, that's a cinch."

"No, but we can wait for the fellow who fixed that grill to come back for his wrist watch. He's sure to do that. By the way, that was a great idea of yours."

"You mean to get his signature? Well, it might come in handy."

"If he's really the man we're after," said Frank. "The joke will be on us if he's not."

After a conference the boys decided to lie in wait behind a large oak tree a dozen yards from the restaurant. No sooner had they concealed themselves than a touring car drove up and several people got out, laughing and joking.

"Nobody there *we* want," Joe whispered.

"No, but here comes another auto with only one fellow in it."

The second car, a small roadster, slithered to a stop not ten feet from their tree. With pounding hearts the boys watched the driver get out. To their dismay he turned out to be a small, insignificant-looking young man.

"Nobody could look *less* like our locksmith," Frank moaned. "Ah, here comes a fellow walking."

"He's a tramp. Bet he won't even stop."

A man in tattered clothing lumbered toward them. Their hearts skipped a beat as he came directly to the oak tree. Frank seized his brother's arm in a warning grip but before either boy could move, the fellow lay down on the ground on the side of the trunk opposite them, stretched himself, and almost immediately began snoring.

Frank grinned sheepishly. "Some detectives *we* are! Getting all fussed over a sleepy tramp."

For nearly two hours the man snored roundly, while Frank and Joe kept up their vigil over the customers of Mike's Munchery. Finally, there being no further arrivals, Frank nudged his brother.

"Guess we're licked for today. Let's go home."

"All right, but I could stand another hamburger first."

Mike fairly radiated pleasure as the boys reentered the roadside restaurant. "You come back for more hamburg', yes?"

Joe nodded. "You bet, Mike. They were wonderful."

The man's eyes suddenly popped. "Oh, I almost forgot. I have news for you."

He dug into a pocket beneath his greasy white jacket and fished out a slip of paper. Frank and Joe watched him in growing anticipation.

"Here," announced Mike triumphantly, handing Frank the slip. "Fellow, he come for watch. I made him sign paper, like you said."

"Jumping salamanders," Joe exclaimed. "How did he get in here, anyhow? How in the name of—" At a warning glance from Frank the lad broke off abruptly.

"He signs himself 'E. Trett'," Frank observed, studying the signature. He looked at Mike narrowly. "Is this the same fellow who left the watch here and fixed your grill?"

The fat proprietor shook his head violently. "No, no, not the same fellow. Another one. A friend."

Frank suppressed a feeling of dismay and ate his sandwich. "Well, I think it's time we got started. So long, Mike."

Outside the shack the brothers looked at each other with mingled astonishment and disgust.

"Wouldn't that make you sick?" Frank

groaned. "I might have guessed our man would send a confederate for his watch. Shucks!"

"I'll bet he was that fellow in the roadster, Frank. All the other customers came in groups."

"You're probably right. Well, there's nothing to do now but go home and see if anything has happened there."

The boys trudged back to Elm Street hardly exchanging a word. Pushing open the front door, Frank uttered a low exclamation and seized a yellow envelope lying on the floor.

"Telegram. Must be from Dad."

"So it is," Joe exclaimed, peering over his brother's shoulder. "He's arriving by plane and pretty soon, too."

Frank consulted his watch. "We haven't much time, Joe. I'll get the roadster."

Two minutes later they were speeding toward the outskirts of town where Bayport's airport was located. Joe, sitting beside Frank who had the wheel, began to write something on a sheet of paper.

"What's that for?" Frank queried.

"Thought I'd try to imitate Trett's signature before we forget what it looks like, Frank. It may come in handy some time."

"Right. Well, here we are. No plane in sight yet."

Frank stopped the car next to a large hangar and the boys hurried out onto the concrete

apron. Just then a loud-speaker blared forth:
"Plane from the West will land in two min-
utes. Incoming passengers will disembark at
Gate Three."

A tiny dot sparkled in the afternoon sun and
a low hum sounded, gradually increasing in in-
tensity. A few seconds later the giant airliner
circled the field, then like a huge bird glided to
a landing.

"Dad'll be the third one off," Joe predicted.
"He always sits in the third seat."

"Don't be too sure about that," his brother
muttered as the passengers stepped down the
gangplank. "Number three doesn't look much
like Dad to me."

The third traveler off proved to be an aged
man with a flowing white beard. He limped
slowly toward the line of waiting taxis.

"Dad's not on the ship, Frank," Joe exclaimed disappointedly as the last person disembarked. "That's queer."

"Maybe there's another airplane due in a
few minutes. This one was full. Oh, Officer!"
Frank stepped up to one of the air line officials.

"No more due till midnight," replied the latter to Frank's question.

Suddenly Joe caught his brother's arm,
"Look, the old man's signalling to us."

Frank turned in time to see a bearded face
watching them from the rear window of one of
the taxis, and a hand motioning.

CHAPTER VII

THE HIDDEN SAFE

"THAT'S Dad," Frank whispered hoarsely. "He's using one of his disguises!"

"Do you think he wants us?" Joe asked as he watched the wrinkled face excitedly.

"I'm not sure. He has stopped waving. Wait here a minute."

Frank started to walk toward the cab. Instantly a deep scowl appeared on the traveler's features and a warning finger came up. The Hardy lad stepped back to where Joe was standing.

"That answers our question, I guess," he said under his breath. "Still, Dad may want us to follow him. Say, isn't that Biff Hooper's car over there?"

A trim blue coupe was parked near the hangar. Inside could be seen an athletic figure apparently watching the small private planes landing and taking off.

"It is, and that's Biff himself inside," Joe declared.

"That gives me an idea," said Frank.

"Whatever it is, we'd better hurry with it. There goes Dad!"

Frank pulled his brother closer. "Listen. Get Biff to drive you after the cab. I'll stay here for a while, just in case anybody is watching us."

"Maybe we'd better just grab another taxi and——"

"No. You can't tell who the driver may be. Hurry up. And make Biff step on the gas."

The younger Hardy boy raced across the apron toward their high school chum.

"Well, I'll be——" began the engaging lad, but before he could finish Joe had jumped in beside him and was issuing orders.

"Sh. No time for questions. Step on it, Biff, and follow that taxicab over there. Quick!"

Young Hooper gave Joe a look of surprise, then sprang into action.

"Nothing I like better'n speed, Joe," he grinned as the engine roared into life. In three seconds the blue coupe was throwing dust behind it in clouds.

"Not too close," Joe warned, pointing at the taxi several hundred feet ahead of them. "Somebody might suspect us."

Biff eased the accelerator slightly and settled back into the seat. "You might tell a fellow what this is all about," he drawled.

"Dad's on another case. He's in that cab, there, in disguise. I want to find out where he's heading. He may need help."

"Don't worry, we'll trail that taxi from here to Siam if we need to," Biff promised.

Joe clutched the back of the seat as they careened around a curve. For a moment the car ahead vanished around a second curve, then appeared again as they gained on it.

"He'll have to slow down pretty soon," said Biff. "We're coming near town."

"Don't lose him in the traffic, whatever you do."

"Say, you don't know me when I'm chasing people," Biff grinned. "I should have been a detective myself."

"Lucky thing you were out at the airport," said Joe. "Frank and I were afraid to trust another driver. Whoa, there he goes toward the waterfront."

The taxi ahead had darted into a narrow side street leading through the slums. For several minutes the two cars wound through the maze of alleys and lanes in the waterfront district, narrowly missing collisions with pushcarts and wagons.

"He's pulling up in front of the Wexel," Biff exclaimed. "Golly, what a place for your Dad to be staying!"

"Better stop here, Biff. Somebody might be spying," Joe whispered.

His chum accordingly drew up alongside the curb nearly a block from the ramshackle hotel where the cab had stopped.

"An old man's getting out," Biff exclaimed. "Say, I thought you said your Dad——"

"He's disguised. Now look, will you do me another favor? Amble over there and see what name he registers under."

"Sure thing, Joe." The good-natured chap hopped to the sidewalk. "See you in a minute."

Tense with excitement, Joe watched Biff lounge up the street and approach the dimly lighted entrance to the Hotel Wexel. The figure of his chum then disappeared. Impatiently the Hardy boy counted the seconds, then the minutes. Several rough-looking men came and went through the entrance. Suddenly a hand touched his elbow. With a suppressed exclamation Joe whirled around in his seat in time to hear a soft laugh.

"Sorry if I surprised you," Biff chuckled. "I figured I'd better come back a roundabout way, just in case. Well, your Dad—or the old man, if he *is* your Dad—calls himself T. H. Armstrong."

"Did he register?"

"Sure did. He got Room 38, dollar-fifty a night."

"Have you any more time to spare, Biff?"

"All the time in the world," replied his chum. "Where to now?"

"Back home. Frank should be waiting for us."

Expertly Biff maneuvered the blue coupe through the winding streets and some time later pulled up to the Hardy home on Elm Street.

Before the boys could jump out Frank had appeared.

"Hello, Biff! What news?"

"Plenty," said Joe.

The three chums hurried inside to Mr. Hardy's study, where Joe related what had happened.

"That's great, thanks to you, Biff," Frank exclaimed. "Now for another quick move on our part. Come on upstairs, Joe."

Leaving their chum in the living room the brothers disappeared, returning a few moments later with two large bundles.

"Well, where to now?" Biff queried amiably.

"Outside of town some place, where we can be sure nobody'll see us."

In a jiffy the three were back in Biff's car.

"How about Mine Hill, fellows? That's pretty well deserted around this time of day."

"Good enough," Frank agreed.

Dusk was falling as they drove into a country road flanked by thick woods.

"This is all right, Biff," said Frank. "Keep watch while Joe and I put on these disguises."

The Hardy brothers quickly transformed themselves with remarkable thoroughness into a pair of slum boys. With shirts and trousers in tatters and faces splotched with dirt they climbed back into the car, tossing their good clothing into the rear.

"Bad as the place is, I don't think even the Wexel Hotel would let you two in," Biff observed doubtfully. "You're *too* filthy looking."

"Don't worry, they'll let us in," Frank laughed.

Retracing their previous journey the boys approached the waterfront again. With pounding hearts the Hardys climbed out of Biff's coupe in an alley several blocks from the Wexel and thanked their chum for his assistance.

"Just give me a ring if you need me," he urged.

"Thanks."

A moment later Frank and Joe sank back into the murky shadows.

"Where are we?" the latter muttered, peering around at the flickering old-fashioned street lamps.

"Tomato Can Alley, I think it's called," said Frank. "The Wexel's about four blocks off that way."

They turned a corner and found themselves in a blaze of lights emanating from a row of cheap dance halls and shops. So rowdyish did the two appear that idlers lounging about paid scant attention to them.

"There's the Wexel," Frank announced.

Instinctively each of the boys drew a long breath. They then headed for the hotel, conversing together loudly in slang. Pushing through a crowd of sidewalk roughnecks cluttering up the entrance they walked to the desk.

"What do you want?" growled the surly clerk who wore gaudy suspenders.

"A room for the night, please," Frank said, speaking hoarsely.

"Oh, yeah?" the man sneered. "Get outa here. This ain't no place for kids."

Frank drew out two one-dollar bills and fingered them significantly.

"Wait a minute," said the clerk suddenly. "Maybe I got an extra room. Yeah, one left. Thirty-nine." He lifted a key from a board. "That'll be two bucks."

Shaking with suppressed laughter the boys climbed up three flights of creaky stairs. As they reached the landing Frank touched his brother's arm and pointed.

"There's Number Thirty-Eight, Joe," he whispered. "Hurray, Dad must be in. There's a light!"

"We'd better go in our own room first," advised Joe. "Get our bearings."

Frank slipped the key into the lock, opened the door and switched on a dim light. After a brief inspection of their unpleasant surroundings they tiptoed into the corridor. They listened for a moment, then tapped lightly on the door of Room Thirty-Eight.

"Who's there?" cackled a feeble voice.

Frank looked at his brother and grinned. "Friends," he said in a low voice.

The creak of a heavy step sounded. A bolt clicked and the door came open slightly. A bearded face looked out at them for a long moment. Then came a chuckle.

"Come in, you two young rapscallions!"

"Hello, Dad," the boys exclaimed softly as they entered and fastened the door.

Smiling broadly, Fenton Hardy doffed his flowing beard. "I'm glad you came, boys. We've plenty to do, so let's not waste time."

Frank nodded. "We're ready, Dad."

"I'm on the trail of a man who is registered here under the name of A. Cole," the detective said under his breath. "He's just across the hall; in fact, in Room Thirty-Seven. I want one of you to get me a dictaphone tonight so I can wire his room before he comes in. He's at the movies now, I happened to find out."

Joe volunteered. "I can be back in an hour with an outfit."

The detective and Frank waited until the younger boy had disappeared, then Mr. Hardy turned to his son. "When Joe returns I want you two to go home for the night and come back in the morning with certain papers in my private safe. They're marked with these numbers," and he handed Frank a slip of paper.

"Anything else, Dad?"

"Yes. Take these letters to my office very early. And by the way, it's high time you were out West hunting for that training camp for spies. You can start day after tomorrow on the *Flying Express.*"

Frank's eyes lighted with pleasure. "That's great, Dad. We'll find the place if it's the last thing we do."

"Well, I hope it won't be. Now, about this man Cole. He is, I have reason to believe, a member of the spy ring. The school is only part of the big scheme."

Fenton Hardy leaned toward his son and talked earnestly for nearly an hour. Suddenly there was a tap at the door and Joe came in with a bulky package.

His father beamed. "Good work, Joe. Now we'll have to hurry. The movies will be over in about twenty minutes."

Expertly the boys went to work, first opening the flimsy lock on Room Thirty-Seven with a piece of wire. In exactly fifteen minutes and just as a heavy footstep sounded on the staircase, they returned to Mr. Hardy's room, grinning triumphantly.

"That's he, all right," said the detective, listening intently. "Very well, you'd better go now."

Next morning the boys were up early. After breakfast they delivered the letters to their father's office, then returned home to get the papers their parent wanted. The front door was not bolted on the inside, so they let themselves in with a key.

"Aunt Gertrude must be out shopping," said Frank as they noticed she was nowhere about.

"It's just as well," Joe observed. "She might ask too many questions while we're getting those articles from Dad's private safe."

"That's one thing about this house she

doesn't know," added Frank. *"And she and
no one else ever must find out the important
hiding place."*

The boys proceeded to the bedroom, closed
the door, and quickly shifted certain stacks of
sheets and pillow cases in the closet. So in-
tent upon their task did they become that
neither heard a creaking sound on the third
floor staircase as a figure hurried down.

"It's burglars this time for certain," quaked
Aunt Gertrude's voice, as she reached the first
floor. "Oh, dear, where is that telephone?
Hello, Operator? Send the police, right away!
Yes, burglars are in the house. Yes, Twenty-
Three Elm Street."

The trembling figure sank into a chair, panting excitedly. The minutes rolled by. Suddenly a car slid to a stop in front of the house.
A moment later two burly officers pushed open
the front door.

"Burglars, you say, Ma'am?" inquired one
in a hushed voice.

"Oh, bless my soul, they're ransacking the
house at this very moment! I was straightening
some things in the attic and I could hear them
in our linen closet! Oh, Officers, please——!"

Aunt Gertrude's hysterical wail broke off as
the policemen pushed past her. With revolvers
drawn they hurried up the staircase.

CHAPTER VIII

"CAN you find the right papers, Frank?"

"I guess these are the ones. Point your flash-light a little to the left, Joe. Yes, here they are."

The older lad handed a batch of documents to his brother, who stuffed them into his jacket pocket. Quickly the boys clanged shut the safe door, closed the panel, and replaced the linen on the shelf.

"Frank! Somebody's coming upstairs," Joe warned his brother.

"Raise your hands!" barked a sudden command as the bedroom door opened.

The brothers stopped in their tracks just out-side the closet. There was a moment of silence, then a familiar cap with visor poked itself from a corner of the hallway, followed by the large nose and jutting chin of——

"Sergeant Boles!" Frank squealed, bursting into laughter.

"Well, I'll be blasted," wheezed the officer, whom the boys had known for many years. "So *you're* the thugs we're after!"

60

The two men looked at each other, then at the boys. All four burst into a fresh round of laughter which was suddenly interrupted by a shrill cry downstairs.

"That must be the lady who sent for us," said Sergeant Boles.

Aunt Gertrude herself appeared just then, peering uncertainly at them. "Why—why, where are the robbers?"

"Right here, Auntie," Joe replied with a serious face.

Their relative's expression changed from one of alarm to a deepening scowl. "I declare," she snapped, "a body would think you boys would let someone know when you are around, instead of prowling about making strange sounds. Goodness!" With an exasperated shrug she flounced off.

"Well," said Sergeant Boles with a wink, "I guess there's not much for us to do around here, Roberts. Let's get back to Headquarters."

"By the way," Frank interrupted, "you haven't found anybody who fits the fingerprints we showed you, have you, Sergeant?"

"Nary a clue, Frank," returned the officer. "But we're workin' on it. We'll let you know when we get some news. So long."

The boys flopped into chairs for a discussion of the recent humorous mix-up. Joe suddenly looked at his watch and jumped up.

"We better get moving," he said. "Dad wants those papers."

After delivering them, they spent the rest of the day doing errands for their father. As the brothers were ready to start for home Joe remarked:

"The *Flying Express* goes through here in fifteen minutes, Frank. Maybe we'd better go down to the tracks and see if any more packages come sailing off the observation car."

"Wouldn't it be a good idea to go near the trestle and not show up at the same point?" suggested Frank. "Let's take this alley. It's a short cut."

The little-used street led them to a small field filled with tall grass. Crossing this, the brothers reached a growth of shrubs alongside the railroad ties just as the moan of a whistle sounded in the distance.

"That's timing things," Frank chuckled. "The *Flying Express* will be here in two minutes."

"Are you sure we're close enough?" Joe inquired. "I can't see where we are with all these bushes in my face."

"Poke your head out here."

The brothers lay huddled on the ground listening to the rising song of the locomotive wheels on the steel.

"She's coming like a bullet," Joe whispered tensely.

To their astonishment the thunderous roar in their ears suddenly ceased and in its stead came a shrill screeching of brakes. The next thing the boys knew the giant locomotive was sliding past them, its wheels throwing showers of sparks. Then, one by one, the long coaches followed with steadily diminishing speed until with a loud metallic grunt the train came to a dead stop.

"Look!" Joe yelled. "The observation car's right there behind that bush."

"Careful," warned Frank. "Don't take a chance on somebody seeing us."

He pulled Joe back and the two boys listened intently. By lying on their stomachs and peering beneath a large scrub oak they could just make out two persons on the back platform. The muffled sound of the men's voices reached their ears. Then came a clear sentence.

"Heavy boots are needed at the camp, sir. Also, it is desired—that we have—leather jackets and socks of wool."

"Mr. Hunt," spoke the second voice sharply, "we do not speak—of the camp—in public. We——"

The man's final words were lost to the boys as the train gave a violent jerk, accompanied by the grating of couplings, and moved off.

Frank's face was tense. "Did you notice something about that second fellow's voice, Joe?"

"I certainly did. It was our locksmith's!"

"It certainly sounded like him. Still, I'm not sure. Seemed more like an older man's voice, in a way," objected Frank.

"Golly, I'd have given anything to have had a look at his face. It's just as well that we didn't take the chance, though. Might have spoiled everything."

"Did you hear him say 'Mr. *Hunt*', Frank?" Joe queried breathlessly. "Remember those underlined words in that bunch of newspapers? Remember one of the words was 'Hunt'?"

"By jiminy, you're right! Say, I have a hunch we're on the trail of something bigger than we ever thought."

Listening intently for a moment and hearing no suspicious sounds, the boys silently made their way back over the field to town.

"There's another funny thing," Frank mused as they walked through the deep grass. "Did you notice how stilted their language sounded? Sort of like a book?"

"That's just the way that locksmith spoke, Frank. I believe that's a clue. We're beginning to get somewhere now."

"Joe, we'd better hurry back and report to Dad right away. He'll be interested."

Arriving at their parked roadster they jumped in and soon reached home. While Frank waited with the engine idling Joe dashed inside and returned a moment later with the old clothes they had used the night before.

"We'll drive out to Mine Hill and do the same stunt we did last night."

It was late afternoon when a trim roadster pulled up to the curb on a deserted side street in the waterfront district and two rough-looking boys jumped out hurriedly.

"I hope Dad's in," Frank muttered.

"We'll know in a minute," said Joe tensely. "There's our ritzy hide-out, the Wexel," he laughed softly.

In a few moments they were standing at the hotel desk once again, where the same surly clerk confronted them.

"What, you two back again?" he growled, "Got two more bucks?"

Frank drew out two crumpled dollar bills and handed them to the man. "All right, go ahead," said the latter. "Here's your key."

With growing anticipation the boys hurried up the rickety staircase and tapped on the door of Room Thirty-Eight. To their disappointment there was no answer.

"We'll just have to wait," said Frank.

"Let's not hang around up here. How about going outside?"

"All right. Maybe we'll see Dad there."

The front sidewalk was crowded with such a hodge-podge of humanity that the boys could hardly push their way along. Ruffians, vendors, beggars, all seemed to make that district their headquarters.

"Let's have a look around the block," Frank suggested at length.

"Suits me. If the rear of the Wexel is as beautiful as the front we ought to enjoy the view," his brother chuckled.

They rounded the corner and were proceeding casually when Joe suddenly stopped short. "Frank! Look over there!"

He indicated the rear fire escape of the Wexel Hotel, which could be seen rising above the roofs of adjoining buildings. At that instant the figure of a man could be seen furtively climbing the steep iron ladder. Every few seconds he paused, peered about, then resumed the ascent.

"Maybe he's just a workman," said Frank.

"I doubt it. Look at him slinking along up there. Say, if I have my altitudes correct he's stopping on the third floor level!"

Frank's pulse quickened. "Stand guard here, Joe. I'm going inside and see what's up."

Just before he reached the third floor landing he halted and listened. Unmistakable sounds of someone creeping along the corridor drifted down to him. His heart skipped a beat as he heard the creak of a door slowly being opened.

"I'd better see which room he's entering before I lose him," Frank muttered to himself.

Taking advantage of the murkiness of the staircase and corridor he stole upward three more steps, then flattened himself against the wall. He could just discern a figure crouching in front of Room Thirty-Seven.

The door was already partly open. The figure hesitated, peering about. For one frightening second Frank thought he had been seen, but the man turned toward the door again, pushed it the rest of the way open and disappeared inside.

The Hardy boy strained his ears as a faint rustling noise came from the room. Bureau drawers were being opened and shut hastily. Suddenly the door creaked open again. The man cast a quick look up and down the corridor, then emerged, carrying a small satchel. He tiptoed toward the fire exit.

For a second Frank hesitated. Should he join his brother and seize the man as he left the building, or should the police be summoned? Inasmuch as the boys had no real evidence against the fugitive, Frank decided on still another plan. Turning on his heel he bounded down the stairs.

"A man just left Room Thirty-Seven with his baggage by way of the fire escape," he announced to the clerk in a low voice. "Maybe he has stolen something!"

The fellow's customary look of annoyance instantly gave way to a scowl. Quickly he vanished into a near-by room marked "House Detective," returning a moment later with a hard-bitten man wearing a badge.

"The fire escape, you say?" the officer demanded of Frank.

Without waiting for an answer he rushed outside and darted into an alleyway with Frank at his heels. Just as they reached the rear of the hotel Joe darted from behind an outbuilding and tackled a man who at that instant had dropped from the last rung of the iron ladder.

"All right, son, much obliged to you," said the detective to Joe. He snapped a pair of handcuffs on the would-be fugitive, a lean, hawk-nosed man who eyed them sullenly. "Now let me have your names, boys," the officer went on.

The Hardys did not wish to give their names, so they just laughed and said they were glad to be of service. The brothers then decided that the sooner they communicated with their father, the better. Accordingly they returned to his hotel room. After an hour's wait Joe suggested that they go home. To their chagrin Fenton Hardy was sitting in his study. He listened intently as Frank related what had happened.

"I must congratulate you both and prepare myself to be overshadowed by my two sons," the detective chuckled when he had heard the story. "The man you caught is the gentleman who registered as Mr. A. Cole at the hotel. As a matter of fact, I was well on his trail when you boys outdid me. I knew he was going to catch the five-fifteen train, and I had a detail of police at the station ready to pick him up. Fortunately you boys saved us the trouble."

"We still haven't told you everything, Dad," said Joe excitedly.

The younger lad went on to relate their ex-

perience with the *Flying Express*. Mr. Hardy
listened with amazement and delight etched on
his strong features.

"Boys," he said tensely, "you've found a
clue that we can't afford to lose. *You must
catch that train* Mr. Hunt is on!"

CHAPTER IX

"THERE's only one way to catch that *Flying Express*," Fenton Hardy finished significantly.

"By plane," Frank exclaimed. He rushed from the room and came back with a large railroad map which he spread out on his father's desk. "Let's see where the train is now on its way west."

Joe looked at the clock and then at the timetable. Mr. Hardy already had the airport on the phone. Then the three consulted.

"There's a plane in the morning which stops at Bainville," said the detective. "That's your best place for getting on board. At that point you'll have time to spare, and it's the express stop this side of Saddler. If your clues mean anything, and the men on the train are spies, they'll probably get off at Saddler."

"Maybe I'd better phone Chet and ask him to drive us to the airport," the younger lad suggested. A moment later he had the fat boy on the wire.

"Take you to the airport?" drawled Chet. "Sure thing, I'll be over early. Remember,

70

though, I don't want to get mixed up in detectiving!''

By the time the brothers had finished eating and packing in the morning Chet was waiting for them. Mr. Hardy summoned his sons into his study for a last-minute conference.

''Remember, boys, *somebody* on that train undoubtedly is on his way to the spy camp we're interested in. I need not tell you again how vitally important it is to the Government that you find the place.''

''We'll find it or bust in the attempt,'' Frank promised.

''And we don't intend to bust, either,'' added Joe with a grim laugh. ''So long, Dad. You'll hear from us soon.''

Waving a cheery good-bye they jumped into Chet's car and sped off toward the airport. A scant ten minutes before the plane was due to take off they pulled up beside the hangar.

''Plane Number Six. All aboard, please,'' droned a voice through the loud-speaker at the entrance gate.

''Come on, we'd better get our tickets,'' said Frank, tugging at his brother's sleeve.

Leaving Chet for the moment they hastened inside the administration building. When they emerged again the ship's twin engines were rumbling already.

''Right this way, please,'' said an attendant.

Suddenly Joe was knocked rudely aside as a thickset man bearing a small package rushed past them and vanished inside the cabin of the craft. Joe recovered himself and stared after the newcomer with an expression of alarm.

"Frank!" he whispered excitedly. "That was our locksmith!"

"I recognized him," Frank exclaimed under his breath. "Say, if he's going to be on the plane, it's too good to be true. We'd better——"

Before the boy could finish the man rushed out again, this time minus his bundle. Without so much as glancing in their direction he hurried toward a line of parked autos.

Frank seized Chet's plump arm. "Do us a favor," he urged in a hoarse whisper. "Trail that fellow. Don't let him get out of your sight. Find out where he goes and report to Dad!"

An attendant stepped up. "The airplane is leaving, sir," he announced to Frank.

Waving to their chum who stood blinking uncertainly at them, the boys quickly stepped aboard and settled themselves in the only vacant double seat. With a dull thud the door closed and the huge ship started down the runway.

"I hope Chet understood what I said and *does* it," said Frank grimly. He peered out the window hoping to catch a glimpse of their chum as they raced by.

"Can you see him?" Joe asked, gazing over his brother's shoulder.

"Too late now," Frank muttered as they soared away. He settled himself deep in the seat and put his lips to his brother's ear. "When you get a chance, walk up and down the aisle and see if you can spot that package."

Joe nodded as Frank turned toward the window and began watching the panorama unfolding below. Little did he suspect that if he had been able to direct his gaze downward past the tail of the ship he might have seen two cars racing along a bumpy country road.

"Wish that fellow would hit a *big* bump and break a wheel or something," Chet was grumbling between clenched teeth as he gave his engine still more speed.

The auto ahead swerved suddenly, then made a sharp right turn into a narrow lane. Chet applied his brakes, slithered halfway around in the dust and took after the fugitive with renewed determination.

"Wish Frank and Joe would chase their gangsters themselves." the stout lad muttered with a deepening scowl. "This is no job for *me*." The boy's actions belied his words, however, for gradually he was gaining on the other car. Then, without warning, the first machine threw up a cloud of dust and screeched to an abrupt stop. Only by swerving and narrowly missing a ditch alongside the road was Chet able to avert a collision. A heavy, scowling fellow stepped out and walked over to Chet.

"Perhaps you will inform me—of the reason

—for which you chase me," he said in an unpleasant voice.

"Who, me?" Chet blinked innocently. "Why, I, uh, I——"

"If not," continued the other with a malicious look, "perhaps you will inform me—concerning the destination of—Frank and Joe Hardy."

Chet gulped. "Why, uh, I don't know, really I don't. They just started for, well, they——"

There was a sickening crunch as the man's huge fist crashed against Chet's double chin. The lad crumpled unconscious in his seat.

"Perhaps that will teach *you* a lesson," hissed the man venomously. He gazed at the still form and the tiny trickle of blood oozing from Chet's mouth. "Perhaps your friends will have *their* lessons taught before long," he finished. Turning on his heel he strode back to his car and sped off.

At that very moment Joe was resuming his seat beside Frank some ten thousand feet in the clouds.

"I can't get a word out of that fellow," he whispered. "He's about as friendly as a sick clam."

"Where's the package?" Frank asked eagerly. "What does it look like?"

"He's holding it on his lap. Can't tell from the shape what may be in it."

"I hate to get off the plane without knowing where he's going," said Frank. "Still, we

have to catch that *Flying Express* at Bainville.''

''Suppose I have a try at him. I'll ask him
if he'd like to read the magazine we brought.''

Before Frank could pull himself out of his
seat the electric sign at the front of the cabin
flashed on, ''Fasten Seat Belts.''

''This must be Normansburg,'' Joe remarked, consulting an aerial map in the seat
pocket.

The boys fastened the safety devices. The
great ship dropped its nose and glided to a
perfect landing.

''Ten minutes' rest,'' announced the hostess,
opening the door.

One by one the passengers rose, stretched,
and filed out—all except a slim young man three
seats ahead of the boys.

''Shall we stay here and watch him?'' Joe
whispered.

Frank nodded and the Hardys pretended
to read. Just then a uniformed messenger
stepped into the plane and exchanged a few
words with the hostess.

''You will find him in Seat Four,'' the boys
heard the woman say.

The messenger handed a telegram to the occupant who held the mysterious package in his
lap.

''Oh, thank you,'' said the man in a startled
voice.

''Ahem!'' Joe cleared his throat loudly. ''I

think I'll have a look inside the pilot's cabin,
Jack." He winked at Frank as he went up the
aisle. At the door of the control room he turned
and smiled at his brother.

"Come on up and have a look at all these
gadgets," he called.

Frank marched up the aisle after Joe. The
two stood peering into the compartment, apparently discussing with great eagerness the
array of dials and meters on the instrument
panel.

"That man was grinning like a Cheshire cat
while he was reading that telegram, Frank,"
Joe whispered. "I had a good view of his face
when I looked back at you."

"Wonder what it's all about," Frank
grunted. "It seems as if we'll have to do some
tall sleuthing to find—" The lad gave a sudden start as someone tapped him on the arm.

"Pardon me, boys, perhaps you can tell me
something about the operation of the plane,"
purred a suave voice.

The brothers whirled about in surprise to see
the young man from Seat Four beaming at
them.

"Why, of course," replied Frank, erasing
his look of astonishment. "Let's see, where
shall we start?"

"Nearly anywhere would suit me," said the
stranger amiably. "I am ignorant about flying
mechanisms. What is that group of levers
for?"

"Those are the throttles," Frank explained. "One for the left engine, one for the right, and a master control lever for——"

"Please be seated," interrupted the hostess just then. "We are ready to take off."

"Thank you for your trouble, young men," said their new friend, smiling broadly. "I shall be pleased to have you continue your lecture at our next stop, if you will be so kind?"

"We'll be glad to explain whatever we can," Frank replied.

The Hardys returned to their seats as the other passengers began filing aboard. Then the two pilots appeared and a moment later the great air liner roared away again.

Frank looked at his brother. "What do you think of that?" he asked quietly with a wry smile.

"Looks mighty fishy to me," Joe whispered back. "Something in that telegram certainly made him friendly all of a sudden."

The brothers sat without speaking for several moments as the engines droned on monotonously. Then Joe nudged Frank. "I'll make a bet with you," he said softly.

"I'm on. What is it?"

"I'll bet he gets off the plane when we do— at Bainville."

"It's no bet. I think he will too!" said Frank. "Joe, we'll figure this thing out if it takes all night. Let me out a minute. I want to talk to that fellow."

As luck would have it, Frank no sooner had left his seat and started up the aisle when the electric sign at the front of the cabin flashed its warning again. Impatiently the boy resumed his seat and began fastening his safety belt.

"Perryville," Joe said, looking at the map again. "Golly, this plane stops at every double house twice."

The drone of the engines subsided to a heavy swish. There was a slight thump as the landing wheels touched the runway. A moment later they rolled to a stop.

"Ten minutes at Perryville," announced the hostess, opening the door. Before any of the passengers could leave, she was presented with an envelope by a messenger. In a moment she tapped Frank on the shoulder.

"Mr. Frank Hardy? Telegram for you."

With mixed feelings of excitement and apprehension the boys tore open the envelope and read the terse message within.

''CHET IN HOSPITAL.   SERIOUS BUSI-
NESS.   ADVISE RETURN HOME IMMEDI-
ATELY.''

CHAPTER X

JOE DISAPPEARS

THE boys looked at each other aghast. Then Frank pointed a finger at the word 'Father' at the end of the telegram.

"I don't believe he sent it," he said grimly. "He always signs himself 'Dad.' "

His brother agreed. "It isn't like Dad to send for us in the middle of an important trip, either, no matter what has happened."

"Still, maybe something terrible *has* happened to Chet."

"I certainly hope not, Frank, but surely Dad can handle things without us." Joe scratched his head thoughtfully. "No, there's something decidedly queer about that wire."

Several passengers jostled them as they disembarked for the ten-minute rest period.

"He's still there," Frank whispered, nodding toward the mysterious occupant of Seat Four. "Guess he's waiting for the next installment of our lecture."

"We'd better make up our minds what we're going to do," said Joe. "If we go back home we'll lose both our men; the one here and the one on the *Flying Express*. If we go on we may be violating Dad's orders."

79

Frank glanced at his watch, then leaned close to Joe so his whispered words were barely audible. "You go ahead with the lecture while I telephone home. We've still eight minutes."

Joe nodded as Frank hurried off the plane and went into a phone booth in the airport building.

"I'm sorry, the line is busy," said the voice of the operator after Frank had given the number. Fretfully the lad waited.

"Plane Number Six for the West, now departing. All aboard, please," called the platform announcer outside.

Desperately Frank signalled to the phone operator but to no avail. He heard the starting cough of the plane's engines. Suddenly he spied a familiar clerk standing behind the ticket desk. In a twinkling Frank was at his side.

"Well, for goodness' sake, if it isn't Frank Hardy," exclaimed the agent. "Haven't seen you since I worked at the Bayport Airport. How——"

"Can you do me a favor, Harry?" Frank interrupted breathlessly. "It's urgent."

"Why not?"

"Hold the ship for a couple of minutes. I have an important call to make and the line's busy."

He gazed eagerly at his old chum whom, as Fate would have it, he had met at this crucial moment.

"I think I can arrange that, Frank." The man left his desk and hurried through an adjacent doorway. A few seconds later he was back. "All right, Frank, make it quick, though."

With palpitating heart the Hardy boy dropped a coin into the phone again and gave the number. Seconds passed; then to his delight and relief he heard his father's stentorian voice on the other end of the wire.

"Hello? Hello, Frank?"

"Haven't much time, Dad," his son blurted out. "We just had a telegram saying that Chet is in the hospital and that we should come home. Did you send it?"

There was an instant's silence on the other end of the line, then, "I didn't send it, Frank, but Chet *is* in the hospital."

"Shall we come home, Dad?" Frank queried with sinking heart.

"Decidedly not," came his father's answer. "Chet's getting along fine."

"We're hot on the track of another fellow. He's on the plane! We don't know whether to follow him through or get off and catch the *Flying Express*."

"You boys separate, if necessary," crackled Fenton Hardy's voice. "Go on *both* trails. Don't lose clues no matter what you have to do."

"All right, Dad. We'll——"

"One more thing. The Government has just

asked me to find out what happened to the Professor Morse you and Joe were telling me about. Seems he was last heard from while travelling on the *Flying Express* a few years ago. Sent a post card from Saddler."

"Saddler!" Frank exclaimed.

The ticket agent tapped on the window. "Make it snappy!"

With an effort Frank controlled his excitement and nodded to the man. "Have to go now, Dad," he said.

"One minute," came his father's voice again. "I'll have a plainclothesman wearing a black and white check tie at each of your other stops. Signal him if you need help."

Rushing from the booth the boy was just in time to get aboard the ship. The hostess smiled chidingly as he slid into his seat.

Joe's wry smile rapidly faded into an expression of keen interest as Frank recounted his talk with their father.

"So we're going to look for Professor Morse too!" he said under his breath.

"Sh!" warned Frank. "From the tilt on our friend's head he may be listening. By the way, how'd you get along with him while I was phoning?"

Joe snickered. "He was kidding us when he said he knew nothing about airplanes."

Frank nodded. "I'm not surprised at that. I *thought* he was just trying to start a conversation."

For a long while the boys remained quiet, reading the magazines they had brought. Suddenly Frank looked up with a start of surprise. "Wonder what *that's* for?" he asked, indicating the electric sign which had just flashed its warning.

"We're not supposed to stop anywhere around here," Joe remarked with a puzzled look.

Just then the hostess tapped Frank on the shoulder. "Have you your safety belts fastened? We are running into a slight weather disturbance."

Frank chuckled and said to Joe, "You'd think we were running into a cyclone to see the expression on our friend's face. Look."

The hostess now was saying something to the man in Seat Four. It was apparent that the 'something' was exceedingly unpleasant to him. His face was contorted with terror.

"He seems to be scared silly over the idea of rough weather ahead," remarked Frank to his brother.

Suddenly the airplane gave a lurch that threw the Hardy boys against each other. A series of violent bumps followed as the ship plunged into a huge cloud mass.

"Look at Mr. What's-his-name, Frank," Joe whispered.

Their mysterious acquaintance obviously was panic-stricken and was peering about wildly. As the boys watched him he suddenly reached into a pocket and began fumbling with some papers.

"He dropped a letter!" Joe exclaimed under his breath. "I don't think he noticed it."

"Or else he's too frightened to pick it up. What I wouldn't give to get hold of it. We might find out his name!"

There was a sudden rat-tat-tat as a burst of rain hit the metal wings of the great ship. Then came a succession of wild lurches and twists that all but took the boys' breaths away.

"What are you doing, Joe?" Frank asked as his brother began unbuckling his seat belt.

Without answering, his brother flipped the ends aside and rose in the swaying craft. Supporting himself with difficulty he made his way along the aisle. He picked up the fallen letter and handed it to the young man. Then he stumbled to his own place.

"What do you think?" he whispered hoarsely. "The letter was addressed to that fellow Trett! Remember? The one who signed the paper for the wrist watch at Mike's."

Frank uttered a low exclamation. "That *is* a clue. Do you suppose this is the same man we saw drive up to Mike's that day?"

"He was young-looking," said Joe. "So is our friend in Seat Four. Considering the letter and putting two and two together——"

At that instant a buzzer sounded three times and a small light flashed over the door to the pilots' cabin. The hostess jostled past them and hurried through the doorway, emerging a moment later with a grim smile on her pretty face.

"The storm is too bad for us to land at Bainville," she announced. "We shall go on to the next regular stop."

There was some grumbling among the passengers, but in the main they did not seem to mind. The brothers realized they had lost their chance of boarding the *Flying Express*. After some time in which the Hardys had nothing but praise for the aviators who were doing a marvelous job in the worst storm the boys had ever been in, the hostess was summoned forward again. After a talk in the control cabin she returned with a dire announcement.

"The pilots are going to attempt an emergency landing on account of the storm," she proclaimed.

At this point the man in Seat Four began tearing up the letter he held into small bits. His trembling hands let the pieces drop to the floor.

"If we crash, he doesn't want anyone to find that message and read it," said Joe tensely.

"Whatever happens," Frank observed, "remember that we're on the trail of that fellow!"

From the pressure on their ears it was evident that they were descending. The plane was rocking madly, and the combined thunder of engines, wind and rain made the boys shudder in spite of themselves.

"A pasture below us, Joe," said Frank

tensely. "I could see it in the lightning."

There was a sudden jolt, followed by another and a third. With a sigh of relief the Hardys knew that they were on the ground. The great ship bounced along for several seconds, then stopped.

Everybody in the cabin heaved a mighty sigh of relief. Suddenly the passenger in Seat Four jumped up.

"Let me out of—this terrible contraption," he exclaimed, running toward the door.

"You had better remain on board, sir," admonished the hostess. "You are perfectly safe here."

"Let me out of—here!" the man fairly screamed.

Flinging the young woman aside he opened the door and jumped into the rain-swept blackness.

"I'll get him back," Joe cried.

In a flash the boy leaped after the fugitive, whom he overtook beneath a large tree. The wind nearly lifted the two young men from their feet. The rain beat into their faces like darts from a blowgun.

"You can't stay here all night," the Hardy lad shouted above the tumult. "Come back."

* * * * *

Inside the plane Frank waited until the excitement had died down and the passengers were busy in conversation. Then he knelt and plucked from the carpet the torn pieces of paper alongside Seat Four. Without letting anyone observe his action he put the fragments into his pocket.

"How soon do you think we'll start?" he asked the hostess who came from the control room at that moment.

The Chief Pilot just behind her stood surveying the passengers.

"Two missing, aren't there?"

"Yes, Captain," the young woman replied. "The man in Seat Four wanted to leave. Another one went out to bring him back."

"Hmph. The storm's letting up. We'll be ready to take off in about ten minutes."

"I'll go look for my brother," Frank said to the attendant, who nodded.

He opened the door and hopped out into the soggy pasture. The wind had begun to abate. Although it was still raining, the sky was clearing in the west. Night, however, already had begun to fall.

"Oh, J-O-E!" he called through the gloom.

Hearing no response, Frank skirted the edge of the field. He was about to enter an adjoining forest when the splutter of engines startled him. Looking toward the plane he saw the hostess framed in the lighted doorway, beckoning to him.

"The pilots say they cannot wait," she said

as Frank hurried up. "They think another storm is coming this way and they must get ahead of it."

The Hardy lad pushed his way up the aisle and went into the pilots' compartment. "Please, sir," he begged the captain, "won't you wait until I can find my brother and the other traveller?"

The aviator shook his head. "Two minutes," he said grimly. "If we don't beat the second storm we'll never make it, young fellow."

Frank turned on his heel and dashed from the plane again. Putting his fingers to his lips he gave a shrill whistle. There was an interval of silence. Then, from somewhere in the thicket near by came the sharp crack of a shot, followed by a blood-curdling scream.

CHAPTER XI

FOOTPRINTS

"WHAT's going on here?"

Revolver in hand, the chief pilot burst through his compartment doorway, strode down the aisle and confronted Frank, who had just re-entered the craft.

"I don't know, Captain," the boy replied tensely. "I gave the secret whistle my brother and I use. You probably heard that shot."

"I certainly did. We'll go and investigate."

They hurried from the plane, walking toward the woods at the edge of the pasture. The pilot switched on a flashlight.

"Footsteps in the mud," said Frank.

His heart pounding lest something might have happened to Joe, he walked rapidly. Suddenly he stopped. In the beam of the flashlight two distinct sets of footprints appeared, diverging from one another.

"Those are my brother's, Captain," Frank exclaimed after a moment's study of the tracks.

The pilot nodded, and without a word they began following Joe's footprints. To Frank's relief they appeared to lead back in the general direction of the plane. Suddenly a slim figure loomed up ahead.

"There he is!" Frank cried. "Joe!"

"Right!" came an answering shout. A moment later the younger Hardy lad came up. "I was just going back to the plane. Somebody shot at us there in that field and Trett or whoever he is ran off."

The aviator gazed at Joe searchingly. "Who did the shooting?"

"I don't know, sir. I thought I saw somebody watching us from behind that ridge. Next thing I knew a bullet whistled over."

The pilot scowled. "Probably some rancher thought you were going to steal his cattle." He glanced at his watch. "All right, boys, let's go back. We won't have time to track down that other passenger."

Soon they were high in the heavens again. The boys settled back impatiently.

"I didn't want Trett to get away from us," Frank exploded.

"Neither did I," replied Joe, "but what could I do? He kept insisting I go to the ship. Said he knew a place where he could get out of the rain."

"Oh!" Frank raised his eyebrows. "He must have been here before."

"Well, anyhow," Joe continued, "he certainly ran off fast after that shot."

"What about the scream we heard?"

Joe shook his head. "Your guess is as good as mine. All I can say is that *I* didn't scream. What do you suppose we'd better do next?"

"We've missed Bainville."

At that moment the hostess announced that they would land at Beegle immediately.

Joe frowned. "We've lost Trett and missed the *Flying Express*. Dad'll sure fire us!"

His brother shook his head. "We haven't spoiled everything yet. We'll get off at Beegle and find the detective Dad said he'd have there. One of us can go with him tomorrow and pick up Trett's footsteps. The other can set up headquarters at a hotel and get in touch with Dad."

"Suppose I go back after Trett," offered Joe.

"All right. Besides, I want a little time to figure something out."

Frank reached into a pocket and brought out the torn scraps of paper covered with handwriting. Try as they might, the boys could get none of the pieces to fit together so the message would make sense.

"Never mind, I'll do it when we reach Beegle," Frank said as the plane began circling for a landing.

"I think I see a black and white check tie," Joe whispered as they stepped out.

"Hullo," drawled a middle-aged man just then. "I'm Kelly. You're the Hardys, I'm thinkin'."

Frank smiled. "Right you are, Mr. Kelly. And we have a job for you."

"Good. Things been dull lately. Come over

here.'' The detective whom Fenton Hardy had stationed at the airport motioned them toward a small coupe. ''Don't mind the old bus, fellows. Roads h'ain't too good around these parts, and she's pretty well shook up. I live about fifty mile from here.''

The three rattled into town and put up for the night in Beegle's Union Hotel. Early the next morning Kelly and Joe sped off alone in the former's coupe. The Hardy boy set a course that would take them approximately to the spot where the plane had made its emergency landing. After an all-day ride, in which the youth changed his mind several times, they found themselves deep in uninhabited country.

''We haven't far to go now, Kelly,'' said Joe. ''I'm sure of it.''

Bang! came a loud report. The car lurched violently, then veered into a shallow ditch.

''Confound it,'' swore Kelly. ''I knew I should o' bought a new tire. No spare, neither.''

Ruefully surveying the ruined flat on a rear wheel they stood for a moment wondering what to do. Finally it appeared that there was no choice but to walk. After an hour's steady trudge they still saw no sign of habitation.

''We should o' gone in the other direction, Joe. Ain't any ranch house around here,'' he added, sitting down.

Joe gazed over the silent landscape in exasperation. Then, leaving Kelly behind, he walked around the next bend. Five minutes

later he was back, grinning. "There's a ranch
ahead!" he informed.

Sure enough, just beyond the turn was a low,
rambling building about a mile from the road.

"Where's all the livestock?" Kelly wondered
as they approached the house. "Some ranch,
'thout any cows!"

Just then the front door swung open and a
plump woman wearing an apron looked at them
questioningly.

"Please excuse our intrusion," Joe said politely. "We had a flat tire and wonder if someone would help us."

"I—I guess so," replied the woman hesitantly. "Just a moment, till I call Mr. Rangle.
Oh, Pete!"

A huge man with a searching face strode out
a moment later. He eyed them minutely.
"Who might you—be?" he demanded menac-
ingly.

When Joe explained their predicament the
man's suspicious expression faded slightly.
"Mebbe I can—lend you a—helping hand."
Then his eyes narrowed again. "Whar did you
say—you're headin'?"

Joe thought swiftly. "My friend and I are
on our way to—to do some exploring. We——"

"We're huntin' for different kinds o' rocks,"
wheezed Kelly blandly. "Geology's my hobby.
Thought mebbe we'd find some quartz crystals,
or dinosaur tracks."

The giant studied their faces for a long moment. Then, in a more friendly tone, he said, "Wal, come along. We shall fetch the truck and—extricate yore auto. We shall fix yore tire with—my vulcanizing machine."

Joe felt a start of recognition at the man's peculiar, stilted speech. Though it was Western in accent, it seemed unnatural to the boy's keen ears. Outwardly the Hardy lad gave no sign of interest, however, and followed Kelly and their host into a barn where a truck was parked.

"Take seats," motioned the big man. A moment later they were rumbling over the lane at a fast clip. "You are geologists?" boomed their host, casting a sidelong glance at Joe, who thought it best to say as little as possible.

"Wal, sometimes you find interestin' rocks around country like this," Kelly interjected, puffing at a large cigar.

Just then the detective's car appeared as they rounded a curve. Rangle pulled up alongside.

"Hm. Exceedingly fortunate—that you did not sever—an axle," he observed. His bookish speech sounded doubly peculiar because of the Western twang that went with it. "Here, take hold of this—chain, please."

Five minutes later they had the auto hoisted up. After a slow trip they arrived at the ranch.

"We'd better start work right away, Kelly," Joe suggested.

"Er, uh, do not concern yoreselves—with it

now," broke in the rancher hastily. "We shall tend to that—later. Supper is prepared."

He motioned them through the back doorway and pointed to three chairs alongside the kitchen table. The stout woman whom they had first met was stirring something in a large kettle on the stove.

"Just sit right down, boys," she said· cordially. "The stew is ready."

In the middle of the meal Rangle laid down his fork and rose. "You—undoubtedly wanta leave—as soon as possible," he said, addressing Joe. "If yore willin' to excuse me I'll go and —repair your tire immediately."

Over the boy's protest he went out. A few moments later the cook Josie too excused herself, saying that she had some chores to do. Left alone, Joe and Kelly looked at each other reflectively.

"What do you make of it?" the detective asked at length.

After a furtive look around at the doorways, Joe remarked, "We're not more than a quarter of a mile from where the air liner landed."

"That so?" Kelly raised his eyebrows. "You think maybe this big fellow's the one that took a potshot at you and your man Trett?"

"He might be," Joe replied tensely.

"Wal, there's one thing sure, and that's this," Kelly remarked. "I've seen plenty o' ranches in my time, but I never heard tell o' one that didn't have no animals on it. Listen. Do you hear any chickens or steers a hollerin'?"

"There's not a sound anywhere."

"What's more, did you see any cowhands around, Joe? I tell you, this is the queerest dump I ever heard of. Must be somethin' goin' on here that we ought to know about."

Joe had a hopeful feeling that his companion was right. In the meantime he decided that it was high time they were moving on. Motioning at Kelly he went outside.

To their astonishment there was no sign of their host, but the flat tire had been fixed. On impulse Joe climbed into the detective's car and tried the starter. There was a whirring sound, then silence.

"Wait a minute, Joe," Kelly said, stepping up and raising the engine hood. "Look here. Gas line's sheered clean off at the carburetor."

The boy stared at the damaged part. "Falling into that ditch never did *that,* Kelly."

"I'll say not. There's only one way that could o' happened. Somebody's cut it, and here he comes now."

The strange rancher was walking toward them from one of the barns. He looked at the raised hood, then at Joe. "What's happened? Does yore motor—refuse to—function?"

Joe nodded and the giant drew a hand across his stubbly chin. "Unfortunate! Wal, you will remain overnight, then? In the morning we shall—arrange repairs."

There was no alternative but to accept the mysterious man's invitation, though Joe chafed at the delay. A single rainstorm, for one thing, would obliterate Trett's footprints and ruin all chances of following the fugitive. A few moments later Kelly and Joe found themselves in a large bedroom. Their host set down a sputtering candle.

"Have a good sleep," he said in what Joe thought was an ominous tone.

His heavy footfalls echoed away in the house. For a long time the Hardy boy lay awake listening to Kelly's heavy breathing, wondering what the morrow would bring. Suddenly he heard a distinct *creak* outside the door. There was a long interval of silence, then another *creak*.

Joe held his breath and listened, his heart pounding. An instant later the door swung open slowly. A menacing figure stood dimly outlined in the pale rays of the full moon.

CHAPTER XII

THE CLUE IN THE ASHES

FOR an instant Joe debated whether or not to tackle the intruder. Before he could decide he recognized the man as the rancher. The huge body was moving stealthily toward the chair where Joe had laid his clothes.

Joe smiled to himself. "Good thing I didn't leave anything in my pockets." Beneath the back of his head he could feel a hard lump where he had placed his money and papers under the pillow.

Pete Rangle had reached the chair and was silently fumbling with Joe's trousers. Next he picked up the boy's jacket. Finally he tossed both garments down again with a muttered "Agh" and stole from the room.

Kelly's heavy breathing, Joe noticed, had stopped. "Say!" the lad whispered. "Are you awake?"

"Sure am. Been watching our pal. Don't think he made out so well."

Joe chuckled. "He certainly didn't. I took everything out of my pockets."

"Purty good for an amateur," Kelly yawned. "I never took my pants off in the first place.

Anybody wants to steal 'em got t' steal me first.''

The detective turned over and began snoring. Joe lay awake listening intently but heard nothing unusual. Finally he, too, fell asleep. When he awoke the sun was streaming in brightly.

"About time you came to," Kelly smiled. He stood in front of a mirror combing his hair. "Remember. Poker faces when we go downstairs," he whispered. "We don't want 'em to catch on that we know what happened last night."

In a few minutes they descended into the kitchen, where Josie gave them a cordial greeting from her post at the stove. As Joe had suspected, the big rancher was nowhere in evidence.

"He's gone to town, boys," the woman said above the hiss of eggs and bacon in the frying pan. "Gone to get some parts to fix your bus with."

Joe and Kelly exchanged meaningful glances, then wasted no time in seating themselves as Josie filled their plates.

"The big fellow—Pete—he's your husband?" Kelly queried between gigantic mouthfuls.

"Yes," said the woman without a smile.

Just then a clatter of hoofs sounded outside the kitchen window. A swirl of dust filtered in, followed an instant later by a thin, swarthy fellow in faded riding clothes. Scarcely glancing at Joe and Kelly he dropped into a rickety chair and propped his feet on the stove.

"Hello, Jake," Josie greeted. "Have some breakfast?"

"I—have just—concluded breakfast," replied the man in a hoarse, unpleasant voice.

Once again Joe gave a start at the familiar stilted speech. The man pulled out a knife and stick and began whittling.

"Mind you don't spill them shavings all over the place," said Josie.

"They will not—harm anything," grunted the visitor.

Without looking up, Joe could feel the scrutiny of the newcomer. For several moments there was no sound save that of shavings hitting the floor. Finally Jake spoke.

"You strangers do much riding?"

Joe saw the man's beady eyes fastened directly on him. "Oh, a little, now and then," he replied casually.

Kelly shifted his chair and peered from the window. "Nice lookin' hoss you have there," he commented.

"Would you—care to—see some—fancy riding?" Jake asked.

Joe and Kelly followed him outside, where a glance told the Hardy boy that the man's horse was, indeed, a good one. Jake vaulted into the saddle, jerked the beast to its haunches, and lunged off in a wide circle.

"Look at him saw those reins," Joe exclaimed

disgustedly. "There's no excuse for treating an animal that way."

"Shore ain't," Kelly agreed with a frown. "Thinks he's all-fired smart."

The rider now commenced a series of acrobatics while the horse raced round and round. Leaping from its back he ran alongside the animal, then jumped into the saddle again, finally ending his exhibition by standing on his pet's haunches at full gallop.

"He's no cowboy, that's sure," Joe muttered as Jake seated himself again and came toward them. "He acts like a trained circus performer."

"And I'll tell you something else," said Kelly, as the man now rode stiffly past them, looking neither to right nor to left. "He shore ain't from around here. You can tell by the way he sits. He rides more like an army man, and a foreigner at that."

Just then Jake pulled up and dismounted in a flurry of lather.

"You shore made him sweat," Kelly observed with a dark look.

"I did not hurt him, he's tough," snorted Jake. "How did you like the—show?"

"Wonderful," returned Joe with an obvious note of sarcasm in his voice. "Let's go inside and take it easy till Mr. Rangle gets back with the parts for your car."

"Good idea," said the detective, catching the boy's wink.

They headed for the house. Jake, after tethering his horse, loped after them.

"I—think I shall—join you," he said, smiling.

He followed them inside and sat down by Kelly in front of the living room fireplace. Joe casually picked up a magazine, while the detective fell into a conversation about horses with their unwelcome guest.

Suddenly Joe's eyes narrowed. He was looking into one corner of the fireplace. For a moment he stared intently.

"You shore don't know horses if you say a thing like that," Kelly was denying emphatically.

"Maybe I've been riding since before you—left your crib," snapped the other.

Joe was now looking hard at Kelly. The detective turned his head and caught the boy's eye. The Hardy lad made a slight gesture with one finger, which the man understood at once.

"I'll prove it to you," the detective said loudly, turning back to Jake. "We'll go outside and have another look at yore nag. I'll show you those shoes don't fit his feet."

"*Feet,*" snorted the other. "Where'd you get that name for hoofs? Where'd you——"

His rasping voice trailed away as the two men went outside. Joe knelt before the fireplace ashes and pulled out a half-burned envelope from one corner.

" 'E. Trett'," Joe exclaimed to himself, staring at the handwriting.

Deftly he flipped out the contents, half of which were burned.

"Hm. Baldon Arms Company," he muttered, studying the letterhead. "Let's see." He began reading. " 'This is to advise . . .,' shucks, next part's burned . . . 'shipment will be sent when vacations begin. Signed Donner, Secretary.' " Joe scrutinized the sheet. "Wish I could make out that first paragraph. Maybe I can see the writing through the scorch. 'Dear Mr.——' "

Footsteps sounded on the front porch. Hastily Joe stuck the remnants of the letter back in the envelope, and threw it into the fireplace. He had just opened his magazine again when Kelly and Jake marched into the room.

"Is there any good drinking water around here?" Joe asked on a sudden impulse, looking at Jake.

"You'll have to—fetch it—yourself, young fellow," the man grunted. "Out in the well."

Seizing the opportunity Joe slipped from the house. From sounds in a room off the kitchen he decided Josie was scrubbing clothes. There was still no sign of Pete. Quietly the boy went to Kelly's auto, flipped up the hood, and began working feverishly. A quarter of an hour later he put down the cover again.

"Are you two still arguing?" he laughed, returning to the living room.

Scarcely had he returned when he heard the sound of an engine.

"Here comes Pete," said Jake.

The giant rancher strode in a moment later, nodding curtly toward Joe and Kelly. "Hello, Jake. Been here long?" he asked.

"Approximately—since you left."

"Good. You are leaving soon?"

Jake stood up and marched off without another word. There was a clatter of hoofs, then silence. Rangle stroked his prickly chin and regarded his two remaining guests thoughtfully.

"I had to order the parts—for yore car. You will have to—stay till morning."

As he turned on his heel and disappeared, Joe quickly told Kelly about the letter in the fireplace. "And thanks for keeping that fellow engaged," he whispered. *"I fixed the car."*

The detective's eyebrows arched upward. "Good work, Joe!"

"It'll last for a while, anyhow. We'll be able to get away tonight. My father ought to be told as soon as possible what we've found out."

"Shore thing. Meantime we'll just hang around and not look or act suspicious."

During the afternoon they lounged about. After supper, just as dusk was falling, Joe began yawning.

"I believe you should—retire," suggested the rancher.

"Guess I might as well."

Bidding their host good night, the two visitors lighted candles and went to their room. Methodically Joe removed his valuables and put them under the pillow, while Kelly flopped into bed, fully dressed.

"What time shall we leave?" whispered the detective. "Why don't you stay dressed?"

"Rangle might come in again. He'd be suspicious if he didn't see my clothes on the chair. We'd better not try leaving before two or three o'clock."

"Well, wake me up. I'm going to catch a few winks."

Half an hour passed. Suddenly Joe heard a rustling sound outside his window. Before he could investigate he heard the unmistakable rumble of conversation in the living room.

"Kelly! Are you awake?"

"Shore am. Sounds like more guests."

"Trett's out there, sure as we're alive. I could recognize that voice anywhere."

The murmuring went on. Silently Joe arose.

"I'm going into the hall," he said.

He paused at the door, listening. Then he twisted the knob.

"Kelly! We're locked in!" he whispered hoarsely.

"What?" The detective eased from bed and tiptoed over. "So we are! All right, Joe, get into your clothes. We'll have to leave by the window, and the sooner the better."

In a jiffy the boy was dressed. It was some time before Rangle and Trett retired. Then Joe peered outside. No one was in sight.

"I'll go first," said the Hardy boy.

Gingerly he climbed over the sill and felt for the ground with one foot.

"Stay where you are!" came a sudden command from the darkness.

CHAPTER XIII

A DARING RESCUE

"WAL, what's on your mind, young feller?"
The clerk at the Union Hotel desk smiled pleasantly at Frank Hardy.

"I'd like to send a telegram," stated the boy.

The man pushed a pad of blanks across the desk to the lad, who thought out carefully how to word a message to his father without giving away the contents to anyone else. Finally he wrote:

'JOE AND FRIEND HUNTING FOR LOST
PLANE PASSENGER. AM STAYING HERE
FOR SPECIAL WORK. HOPE TO HAVE NEWS
SOON. LOVE FRANK'.

Having dispatched the wire, he hastened upstairs to his room. Fishing in one of his pockets he pulled out the scraps of paper he had picked up in the plane and assembled them on a table.

"Now for the puzzle," he said to himself.

For a solid hour he labored intently, trying to make sense of the handwritten words which seemed to consist mainly of numbers and names of persons.

"Shucks," he exclaimed disgustedly at length,

107

"I'm getting nowhere." Suddenly his face brightened. "Maybe if I forget about the text and just try to fit the scraps themselves together——"

He went to work again with a fresh burst of energy. This time his progress was faster. At the end of another hour he uttered an exclamation and stood up.

"There! Everything fits! Now, what's it all mean?"

The boy had pieced together two large sheets of paper, each of which contained a list of proper names. Opposite them were numbers, most of which were in the seventies and eighties. In addition, the second sheet contained a separate list of proper names opposite which were the days of the week. At the bottom of the second sheet, in a space by itself, was the single notation: 9:15.

Another hour went by as Frank puzzled over the strange letter. "Looks like a school report card," the thought occurred to him over and over again. "Maybe that '9:15' is the time the class starts." Then he shrugged. "Shucks, that couldn't be right."

From somewhere below his room came the cheery sound of a dinner gong. "A good idea," Frank muttered. "Maybe a little food will stir up my brains."

A woman at the next table in the dining room started a conversation about the slow service.

She explained that she had left her infant alone upstairs and didn't like to be away from her so long. Frank was polite but talked little as his mind was on other matters. He was just finishing his second lamb chop when he laid down his fork with a clatter that made the waitress start in surprise.

"Is something wrong with the dinner?" she asked.

Frank smiled. "No, it's fine," he said absently. "Let me have the check, please."

Leaving the astonished woman gaping after him the boy paid the bill and hurried into the lobby of the hotel. "Do you happen to have a timetable of transcontinental trains?" he asked the clerk at the desk.

"Why, yes. Here's one."

Fairly bursting with anticipation Frank opened the sheet and scanned the contents for trains coming from the East. "*Flying Express,* where are you?" he muttered to himself. "Ah, here! And you start your Western trip at— at—" he gazed at the fine print in triumph, "—at 9:15!"

He turned and raced upstairs.

"Sure as shooting that's the clue I'm looking for," he thought, sitting down once again before his work table. "These names and numbers have something to do with the *Flying Express!*"

His heart suddenly sank. Perhaps he was

jumping at conclusions. Perhaps the clue was too farfetched. After all, the number "9:15" might mean anything.

"No, I've a hunch it means that the *Flying Express* starts from the East at 9:15," Frank said firmly to himself. "Putting that together with what I already know about that train I *must* be right. Gee, if only Joe were here!"

The excited boy got up and began pacing the room. What more could he accomplish before his brother might return? Suddenly, from somewhere outside his door there was a scream.

"Fire! Help! Fire!"

Frank sprang to the door and yanked it open. The corridor was thick with smoke. Other patrons were already hurrying outside, some crying out in fear, others shouting words of encouragement. The Hardy boy knew that this old tinder box of a hotel would burn in no time.

Rushing back into his room Frank scooped up the scraps from his worktable and stuffed them into his pocket. Then he madly threw his and Joe's clothes into their suitcases and dashed into the corridor. He collided head-on with a frantic woman. She was the one he had seen in the dining room.

"My baby!" she cried. "Oh, save my baby!" Shuddering with terror she pointed toward the end of the hall, which was dense.

"Which room?" Frank gasped.

"The last one!" shrieked the mother.

Frank threw down the bags and darted off.

Holding his breath, he dodged through a doorway. He fumbled blindly until his hand touched what felt like a crib. There was a feeble cry. Through the smoke he saw the infant's eyes blinking and the tiny chest heaving.

In a jiffy he had the child tucked under his coat. As he turned to go there was an ominous splintering sound above him. With a cry Frank charged toward the nearest fire escape just as the ceiling of the room thundered down.

In a matter of seconds the Hardy lad found himself drinking in the fresh, open air of the street, with the child's mother clinging frantically to him. A roar of astonishment went up from the crowd of onlookers as the lad opened his coat and disclosed the infant.

"Oh, my baby!" the woman sobbed. "How can I ever thank you, dear boy!" She took her tiny daughter in her arms, smiling gratefully at her rescuer.

At this moment firemen warned people away. There was no chance to save the old structure— its flimsy wooden walls suddenly collapsed. As Frank gazed at the smoking ruins, realizing his clothes and those of his brother were gone, he wondered what to do next.

"Neither Joe nor Dad will know how to get in touch with me," he said to himself.

His disconsolate look must have been noticed, for a voice at his elbow said, "Howdy, stranger, is anything wrong?"

Frank whirled around to see a lanky, middle-aged man, attired in full cowboy regalia, smiling at him.

"Y—yes, no," replied the Hardy boy. "Lost my clothes in there."

"I'm shore sorry t' hear that," said the friendly native. "Glad t' lend you some o' mine," he smiled, "only I ain't got another whole outfit."

Frank liked the man at once and asked his name. He was startled to be told "Weather-Eye."

"I jest go along givin' advice on what the heavens is gonna do," the cowboy said breezily. "I kin shoot as straight on that as I kin with a gun! Well, so long, pal," he added, "let me know ef you need my help."

Humming a song of the prairie he wandered off up the street. Frank watched the carefree Westerner a moment, then his thoughts turned to his brother. His face took on a determined look.

"I'll have to look for Joe," he said to himself. "He should have been back here long ago. Something must have happened to him. But I better not go alone," he decided. "Maybe I can get a deputy sheriff to ride with me."

He walked rapidly up the street and climbed the steps into the sheriff's office. As he entered a sudden thought came to him. He had almost forgotten one of his missions.

"Well, what's on your mind?" inquired a

red-faced individual wearing a tin star on his shirt.

"I want to inquire about a Professor Morse who disappeared around here a few years ago. He was last heard from at Saddler. Do you know anything about him?"

Frank thought he caught a look of alarm in the other's face. Then the man summoned another officer.

"Wertz, look up a Professor Morse in the files," he ordered. This time Frank distinctly saw the sheriff wink gravely at the second officer.

"There's one more matter I'd like to ask about," Frank began as soon as he had made a mental note of the situation. "My brother went off on a—a camping trip and hasn't returned."

"Well?" grunted the man unpleasantly.

"I think something may have happened to him. I'd like to have one of your deputies go out with me and hunt for him."

"Huh!" The officer threw back his shaggy head and laughed uproariously. "Young feller, do you think all we have to do is go out huntin' for folks? Nope, ain't got time."

Frank reddened violently but held his tongue A moment later the second officer returned "There's a Professor Morse in the files, Chief, but nothing's ever been heard about him."

"All right, Wertz. Well, boy, good luck out there in them thar woods. Look out for b'ars!"

Smarting with rage, Frank turned on his heel and left. Suddenly a familiar figure crossed the street in front of him.

"By golly," the Hardy boy exclaimed to himself, and broke into a run. "Hey, Weather-Eye!"

The cowboy turned around and at once the man's honest face widened in a grin of delight. "Wal, now if 'taint my old pal ag'in!"

"Weather-Eye, how would you like to take a little trip with me?" Frank asked eagerly.

"Allus ready to help out a pal," replied the cowboy, "any place, any time."

"Good," exclaimed Frank. "I'll rent a car and we'll start right away."

Quickly he explained his fears for his brother to Weather-Eye, who showed great concern over the situation and promised to assist in any way possible. Accordingly Frank wasted no time. Almost before the man knew what was happening, the lad had managed to rent a used coupe at a near-by garage.

"Now for a map," he said.

While the garage man was filling the tank, Frank consulted the chart and laid out a course as close to Joe's as he could remember. Then he and his quaint companion drove off rapidly. It was almost dusk when they arrived at a deserted crossroads far in the country. Frank could not make up his mind which one to take.

"Wal, I allus say when you cain't decide, jest look at the sky," said Weather-Eye. "See them clouds thar? Now, see them others over thar? It's a-goin' to rain on the left-hand road fust. Long afore it rains on the right-hand 'un, seein' how they run way apart.''

"Then we ought to take the right-hand one?''

"Shore thing, if we've a mind to keep dry. Take it from me, lad, I ain't never missed a forecast yet.''

With nothing else to influence him, Frank decided to follow his strange companion's advice. The ride was bumpy and monotonous. For two hours the travellers bounced along without seeing a sign of habitation. The cowboy squinted at the huge clouds massing up on the gloomy horizon.

"Must shore be rainin' on that left-handed road by now,'' he mused.

Suddenly Frank let the car slow down. "Lights, Weather-Eye,'' he exclaimed softly.

What appeared to be a rambling ranch house could be seen dimly in the distance.

"Wal, what're we waitin' for?'' Weather-Eye queried. "Yonder's a ranch house or I never saw one.''

"I was just figuring something out,'' he said aloud. To himself he added, "We're close to the field where the air liner landed and Trett escaped. I wonder—I wonder if Joe's in that ranch house!''

CHAPTER XIV

A FIGHT ON THE PLAINS

"ALL right, here we go," said Frank at length.

He threw the car into gear again and speeded up. At that instant the headlights went out.

"Hey, what's happened, lad? We struck blind?" his cowboy companion exclaimed with a start.

Frank fumbled with the switch but to no avail. Suddenly a pair of flickering lights appeared in the distance.

"It's another machine!" yelled Weather-Eye. "Coming this way. It'll hit us!"

A motor which was whining in the distance rapidly grew louder. Joe and the man who was sitting beside him watched as a car shot around a bend in the road. Desperately Frank put on speed and swerved into a field adjoining the highway. He was just in time. With a roar the other vehicle whipped past them and disappeared.

"Whew!" the boy exclaimed. "That was a close one!"

"Too close, I'd say," Weather-Eye agreed. "Pussonly I'll stick to hosses. Much safer."

For an instant Frank wanted to turn around and give chase. Perhaps Joe was in the other car! But obviously it was impossible to drive without lights. To attract attention he banged his fist impatiently on the horn. Nothing happened.

"Weather-Eye, I guess we'll have to poke around this bus until we find out what's wrong. Know anything about electricity?"

"Enough to leave it alone."

With the aid of his flashlight Frank raised the hood and began fussing with various gadgets inside the engine.

"Hi, ho, here's jest what I was prayin' for," Weather-Eye exclaimed. "A hoss!"

Frank looked up to see a white mare not far away. The cowboy tiptoed up to her and held out his hand. "See, lad, she's a friendly critter. She'd like as not——"

Crack! A shot rang out in the night air not far distant. With a loud neigh the horse galloped away, her hoofs thundering on the soft ground.

"Now, wouldn't ye know somebody'd come along and spoil everything?" Weather-Eye moaned.

Frank was listening intently, but there was no further unusual sound. He turned back to his job. So far he had not found the trouble with the lighting circuit. At length he uttered an exclamation of disgust and summoned the cowboy.

"We'll try driving on a little nearer that ranch house, Weather-Eye, and then we can walk the rest of the way."

"Suits me, lad." He settled himself in the seat and began humming.

Frank swung the car back onto the road. It was hard work to keep from going into a ditch, but soon the moon appeared and lighted their path. A short distance from the house he suddenly sat up straight and stopped the machine.

"Weather-Eye, isn't that a man with a rifle sitting over there?" he asked.

In the rays of the moon an open space on one side of the house could be seen easily. It was here that Frank thought he could make out the figure of a man holding a gun.

Weather-Eye clucked his tongue. "Kinda seems as if yo're right, lad. Looks like trouble to me."

Frank hesitated a moment. Finally he turned to his companion. "Come on, we'll slip up there on foot and investigate," he said.

To his delight the cowboy nodded. "I never was a troublemaker, but I ain't one to back out'n danger nuther. Not when a pal needs help!"

Frank switched off the engine and they climbed out of the car. "I think we'll circle around and approach the house from the other side," the boy advised. "No use getting the man with the gun excited too soon."

"That's right," drawled his companion. "Cain't never tell, though. Mebbe he's jest set-tin' there waitin' for stray animals. That might o' been him shootin' a while back.''

"If that's what he's waiting for, we'll know about it soon enough. It's a good thing we have the moon with us. It would be tough going through this thicket otherwise.''

Weather-Eye chuckled. "I knew we'd have the moon, but I didn't say nuthin' 'bout it. Thought I'd surprise you.''

To Frank, the cowboy's simple humor was a welcome relief. The Hardy lad found himself better prepared as a result to face the grim possibilities ahead. For one thing, he was certain that Joe had met with foul play, and he was fairly sure that the next few hours would tell the story.

"Say, this shore be a queer kind of ranch,'' Weather-Eye whispered as they stumbled along. "Not a hoss nor a steer nowhere.''

"Hmph, that *is* strange,'' said Frank.

The two rested for a moment, peering over the moonlit landscape. Not an animal could be seen nor heard anywhere.

"Mebbe it's one o' them newfangled dude ranches,'' Weather-Eye speculated. "All they have is rockin' horses.''

"Don't you believe it,'' Frank laughed. "I've seen dude ranches with more animals than regular ranches. But there's certainly something mighty peculiar about this one.''

There *was* something mysterious about the absolute silence around them. Frank suppressed a shiver and started onward again. A few moments later they reached another thicket that brought them to within a few dozen yards of the outbuildings. Just beyond was the main house, low, rambling, and now utterly dark.

"Guess everybody's asleep," the cowboy suggested.

"Maybe so, and maybe not," muttered Frank. He hesitated for a moment, listening. "I'll tell you what, Weather-Eye. You stay here and keep watch. I'll go around and see what our man with the rifle is doing."

Frank darted from the bushes, flattened himself against the first outbuilding, then advanced cautiously up to the main structure. Hugging the side of the house he made his way toward the entrance. Once he slipped and caught his breath as a loose stone rattled. For several moments he stood stock-still, then advanced again.

Suddenly he heard a queer, scraping sound, which appeared to come from the front of the house. Silently he crawled over the remaining few feet of ground to the corner of the building. Then he gazed ahead.

Over the sill of a window a figure was draped, feet dangling in midair. Frank's heart missed a beat. Something about the person was familiar.

"Joe!" he said to himself.

At the same instant a sharp command rent the night air. "Stay where you are!" came the words.

Frank's eyes darted toward a small tree. There, with rifle aimed, stood a man half-hidden in the shadows.

For an instant the boy's impulse was to dash out and try to tackle the fellow. Immediately he knew that such an attempt would be suicidal. Better to wait and trust to Joe's common sense to obey the command.

Still, something had to be done and done quickly. Taking a chance on being heard Frank turned and raced back through the shadows toward the thicket.

"Weather-Eye!" he called in a loud whisper.

"Here I be, lad. What's to be done?"

"We must make a capture."

"Shore thing. Where do we go?"

"Follow me, and don't make any noise. When I say the word we'll tackle the fellow. Careful, he has a gun."

"Don't worry about that, son. Guns sometimes get turned around backwards."

Smiling at Weather-Eye's quaint way of putting things, Frank turned and led his companion to the edge of the thicket. There he stopped, put his fingers to his mouth, and gave a low whistle which he repeated three times.

"Say, that's good," the cowboy exclaimed. "You sound like a bird and I cain't tell where it's comin' from, nuther. You been studyin' ventriloquism or whatever you——"

"Sh," Frank warned.

He beckoned Weather-Eye to follow him.

Like noiseless ghosts the two wove in and out among the various buildings until they reached the main house. Then the Hardy boy retraced his former steps, with the cowboy close behind him. At the corner of the structure they stopped short. Directly ahead stood the man with the rifle, gazing upward attentively. Frank pointed.

"Ready?" he asked soundlessly.

"Ready," nodded Weather-Eye.

With a simultaneous lunge the two hurled themselves directly at the guard.

CHAPTER XV

THE SECRET PLAN

GRIPPING the man's throat, Frank glanced upward. No one was in sight at the window. He motioned to Weather-Eye.

"Find some rope, quick!" he cried.

The cowboy fished into a deep pocket and brought out a small coil. "Weather-Eye ain't one to come unprepared," he grunted as he trussed up the squirming guard with surprising agility. "Now lend me that bandanna o' yourn," he ordered.

Sheepishly Frank brought out a clean white handkerchief. The cowboy stuffed it into their victim's mouth.

"That'll fix 'im, lad."

"Good. Drag him over there in the bushes, Weather-Eye. I've an errand to do."

As the man marched off with his burden in tow Frank went to the window where his brother had been dangling a few moments before. He gave a low whistle. A few seconds passed, then a face popped into view.

"That you, Frank?" came a hoarse whisper.

An instant later the younger Hardy lad's feet touched ground. Then Kelly appeared.

Skillfully the big man swung himself from the sill and landed with a dull thud.

"Congratulations, Frank," he whispered, giving the boy's hand a squeeze. "You saved the day for us, sure!"

Joe held up a warning finger. "I thought I heard something. We'd better get started. No telling when our friend Pete Rangle will show up."

Cautiously Frank led them across the narrow clearing into the adjacent thicket where Weather-Eye was waiting for them.

"I had to knock him out," muttered the cowboy, pointing at a dim shape lying on the ground a few feet away. "He was gettin' rambunctious."

In a few words Frank told Joe and Kelly his story. "Didn't you have a car?" he added.

The detective nodded. "I *did,* but I don't see it now. It was standing over there under that tree. Evidently somebody has taken it."

"We'll all go in mine," said Frank.

In single file, with the older Hardy in the lead, they hurried through the thicket, scarcely pausing until they had reached the auto. Quickly they piled in.

"Our lights and horn went haywire, so we'll have to get along without them," Frank explained as he started the engine. "This moonlight helps."

"Moon's goin' under a cloud in about fifteen

minutes,'' Weather-Eye prophesied, ''so ye'd better step on the gas.''

A scant quarter of an hour later the moon actually did disappear beneath a mass of clouds. For a time they drove on, with Frank desperately straining his eyes in the inky blackness to keep the coupe on the road. Suddenly Joe uttered a whoop.

''Lights ahead!'' he cried.

''It's another car,'' Frank whispered hoarsely. He jammed on the brakes. ''Joe, have a look up there and see if I can pull into that field.''

His brother hopped out, ran ahead a short distance, then called, ''You can make it.''

The machine swerved and jolted over the rough ground. Then the engine was switched off. Leaving the others, the two brothers crept through the tall grass at the edge of the road to watch the approaching twin lights. The rumble of an engine came closer. Then an auto shot past them, rocking crazily.

''That's Kelly's car,'' Joe exclaimed. ''The one we came in!''

''I can't say I'm surprised,'' the detective remarked at length. ''But don't worry, boys. We'll catch up with those fellows one of these days. Then they'll pay plenty for takin' things that don't belong to 'em.''

He agreed with the Hardys that the matter of the stolen car should be reported to the authorities. Among them they got the lights fixed and started for Beegle where they spent the night at a rooming house. In the morning they went directly to the sheriff's office. Frank's heart sank as he recognized the same indifferent officer with whom he had spoken the day before.

"Wal, what about it?" drawled the man when told about Kelly's missing auto.

"We'd like to have you send some of your men to the ranch to get it back," said Frank.

The sheriff yawned. "Wal, mebbe yo're right, young feller. I'll round up some o' the boys later on."

With that he leaned back in his chair and began to doze. Impatiently Kelly motioned to the others and they filed out.

"If you ask me, there's something fishy about that sheriff," said Joe. "I never heard of a police officer who didn't care a hang when something was stolen."

"Neither have I," his brother agreed, "but that's not going to stop us. In the meantime we have plenty to do."

"If I might make a suggestion," Kelly interrupted, "I'd like to do a little scoutin' on my own. Mebbe I can turn up a few interestin' facts about that crazy ranch we were visitin'."

Frank turned to Weather-Eye. "Maybe you'd like the job of looking for Kelly's car," he suggested.

The cowboy scratched his tousled head. "Suits me fine, lads," he drawled. "Wisht it was a *hoss* 'stead of a autymobile I was lookin' for."

Waving good-bye to their eccentric friend the boys talked over their next move. They decided to go directly to a telephone and communicate with their father. Frank put in the call to Fenton Hardy's office and waited impatiently. Finally he heard the detective's voice.

"Hello, Dad! Yes, we're all right." He gave their new address. "Clues? I'll say so! I pieced together a list of names from some torn papers Trett dropped on the plane and— hello? Hello, Dad?"

Frank could hear strange sounds, then all was quiet. Anxiously he clicked the receiver. There was no response. For several moments the operator tried to get the number again, but in vain. Finally the boy hung up.

"What's the matter?" Joe asked, seeing his brother's frown.

Frank told what had happened. "I don't like it. It almost seemed as if Dad might have been attacked while he was talking."

"Let's stick around, Tom," suggested Joe, "and wait for a telegram."

Worried, the boys began speculating on Joe's experience at the strange ranch.

"Trett's mixed up with it, sure as you're alive," the younger lad decided. "I'm certain

I heard his voice. He must have known he was near that ranch when our plane made that emergency landing. That's why he ran off.''

Since it was necessary for the boys to buy some clothing, they shopped for a while, had lunch, and then went to the railroad station to ask for a telegram. None had come. In disappointment they went back to their rooming house.

Frank suddenly pulled his hand out of his pocket and with it a crushed envelope. ''I'd almost forgotten to tell you about my big discovery,'' he said.

While Joe listened with growing excitement, his brother told of piecing together the scraps of paper with their strange assortment of names and numbers.

''By jiminy, I'll bet you're right about that having something to do with the *Flying Express*,'' agreed Joe. ''I shouldn't be surprised if those fellows on the list were regular commuters!''

Frank jumped to his feet. ''Joe, you've hit it!''

''What do you mean?''

''I mean that's just what those fellows are —commuters. They're agents travelling between their headquarters in the East and the spy camp we're looking for.''

Joe whistled in surprise. ''That's a pretty good theory if we can prove it, Frank.''

''We'll prove it, Joe, one way or another!

Remember I told you about the days of the week that were placed alongside the names of people?"

"Yes."

"If my theory's right the man whose name is listed alongside the word 'Wednesday,' for instance, would travel on the *Flying Express* leaving on Wednesday."

Eagerly Frank brought out the torn scraps again. This time the task of piecing them together was simple.

"Now, let's see," said the older Hardy lad excitedly. "Here's the first name, H. L. Fox. Opposite his name is—Tuesday! That would mean he's aboard the *Flying Express* that will go through here today!"

The boys could scarcely contain themselves in their delight over the apparently correct solution of the puzzle. Then Joe frowned. "We still haven't figured out how to *prove* that Fox is on that train," he stated.

His brother winked knowingly. "Haven't we? Listen to this, Joe. Why not write a fake telegram? One of us will board the *Flying Express* with it. Then, if our man's on the train we'll not only find him, but we'll find out where he's going!"

Joe's answer was to jump up and clap his brother on the back. "Frank, you're a genius! That's the best idea you ever had in your life. Let's plan out the details and get started right away."

Joe borrowed a typewriter from the woman who ran the rooming house. Frank hustled to the station, sent his father a wire, and helped himself to a few blank telegraph sheets. Then, excitedly, the brothers began the task of composing the first fake message, their door locked against intruders.

"I tell you what," said Frank at length. "We'll mention something about supplies."

"That should make it sound plausible," added Joe.

Frank already had scribbled a message. He read the result in a whisper:

H. L. FOX ABOARD FLYING EXPRESS
YOU FORGOT SEVERAL SUPPLY ITEMS. AM
BRINGING THEM ALONG ON NEXT TRIP.

"Whose name are you going to sign, Frank?"

"The first on our list, Joe. Let's see, who is it?" Quickly he consulted the pieced-together scraps of paper. "It's a fellow named J. T. Thorn. He's supposed to take the next *Flying Express*. We'll sign his name, Joe."

The younger Hardy's eyes widened. "I see what you're driving at now, Frank. We'll just run through the whole group one after the other. We'll give them all telegrams, just as fast as we can make the trips aboard the train. Where shall we get on?"

The answer to this took time for their plans had to be laid carefully. Finally it was decided that no doubt the suspected men would get off at Saddler. This was the place the newspapers had come from.

"You catch today's express at Bainville— that's the stop before Saddler, you remember," said Frank, "and try to find Fox. I'll get on tomorrow's train with a telegram for Thorn. We'll do the same with the rest on the list— Waxen, Gamble and the others. Then we'll have evidence on the whole bunch."

In their excitement they did not realize they had raised their voices. Suddenly there was a knock on the door to the hall.

CHAPTER XVI

MUFFLED VOICES

"Who can *that* be?" Joe exclaimed under his breath. "I hope he didn't hear what we said."

"Never mind who it is. We'd better get this stuff out of sight."

Frank swept the telegraph blanks into a table drawer while Joe hastily shoved the typewriter into a closet. Then, with a quick glance around the room, the latter opened the door.

"Greetings," beamed a tall, well-dressed man wearing expensive clothes. "May I have the privilege of entering—your comfortable abode?"

Joe eyed the newcomer hesitantly. "Y-yes, come right in."

"I thank you."

The man stepped inside and bowed formally. Seating himself gracefully, he placed his hat upon his knee with a flourish.

"I shall—come to the point at once. My name is Bumper. I understand—you young gentlemen are from the—East."

Frank felt himself stiffening. He shot a glance at Joe but the latter showed no sign of having recognized the stranger's stilted speech.

"We are from the East," said Frank levelly.

"Good," returned the other. "I think I have a—proposition that may be of—interest to you. That is, of course, if you are not—afraid of work and—danger." He paused dramatically and studied their faces.

Joe glanced at his watch with a start. He must leave at once in order to catch a plane at the Beegle airport to take him to Bainville where he would board the *Flying Express*.

"We're not interested, sir," he broke in. "We haven't much spare time."

A shadow crossed their visitor's face. "You are—quite certain that you can afford to—lose this opportunity?"

"I should say that we can *not* afford to lose good opportunities, sir," interjected Frank with a sharp glance at his brother. "Might we have a few details?"

A quick smile flashed over the stranger's clean-cut features. "I am glad to hear you—say that." He leaned toward them. "As for details, you shall hear them—at the proper time. Just now I wish only your—acceptance."

"You have it," said Frank boldly. "What do you want us to do?"

The man held up a slender forefinger. "Wait," he whispered mysteriously. "Wait—until you hear from me again. It will be—soon." He stood up and bowed stiffly. "And now, I—thank you. I wish you—good day."

He turned smartly on his heel, almost in military fashion, and went out.

"What's the idea? I've only twenty minutes left to catch the plane for Bainville," Joe grumbled, looking at his watch again. "What about those telegrams?"

"We'll write the rest of them in a jiffy. Here are the blanks. Get the typewriter, quick."

It was a matter of only a few minutes to complete their task. Frank counted the messages and gave those for alternate days to Joe, stuffing the rest into his own pocket.

"Good enough," said Joe tensely. "Well, I'd better get started. What are you going to do, Frank?"

"Stay here and try to find out who just called on us. I'll bet he's part of the spy outfit. Tomorrow I'll catch the next *Flying Express* and try our fake telegram plan myself. Good luck!"

Dashing downstairs, Joe got a taxi at a garage and was driven rapidly to the airport outside of town. The plane was in, so he boarded it immediately. In a short time he was at the Bainville field and hurrying by car to the railroad station. He bought a ticket for Saddler just as the *Flying Express* screeched to a standstill. Wishing it to appear that he was rushing aboard to deliver the important telegram at the last moment, the Hardy lad waited with pounding heart until he heard the whistle.

"'Board," shouted the conductor.

Joe rushed from the station and headed for the nearest coach entrance, climbing on just as the train started up.

"Well, you made it," smiled the man in uniform, grabbing Joe's arm and helping him up the steps.

"I—I have a telegram here, sir," the boy panted, handing the envelope to the official. "It's for a Mr. Fox."

The conductor glanced at the typed name. "All right, young fellow, I guess the porter will find him if he's aboard."

The man turned and swayed down the aisle of the coach. Joe, pretending to be looking for a vacant seat, followed at his heels. Just then a grinning, white-coated porter appeared.

"Page this fellow," ordered the conductor, handing over the message and disappearing into the next car.

Joe waited until the porter had started walking down the aisle calling out the name of Fox; then he followed at a discreet distance.

"I hope the scheme works," he muttered nervously to himself.

The porter reached the end of the car without a response, and continued into the next one with Joe not far behind. When they had passed through the entire train with the exception of the last sleeper, the Hardy boy's heart sank. There were only half a dozen passengers in this car.

"Mr. Fox heah, Mr. Fox?" the porter called

above the muffled roar of the wheels. "Is dey a Mr. Fox heah?"

Suddenly a fat, red-faced individual looked up from a newspaper. "Here, boy."

Joe's heart leaped as the man flipped the porter a coin and ripped open the telegram. Fortunately there was a vacant seat just behind him. Into this the boy slipped, trying to appear unconcerned. His pulses bounding, he watched as much of the man's face as he could manage to see.

Apparently the fellow was not surprised at the message. A few seconds after reading it be stuffed the sheet into the envelope, put it into a pocket and turned back to his newspaper.

"Golly, if only Frank could have seen that!" Joe exclaimed to himself, overjoyed.

Lest he arouse suspicion by staring at the man, he spread open a magazine and began reading. Suddenly the seat ahead of him creaked. Cautiously Joe raised his eyes. Mr. Fox had arisen and was seating himself beside a smartly dressed woman near by.

"More clues," Joe smiled grimly to himself. "Trouble is, I can't hear those people."

The boy glanced around, wondering how to get closer without being observed. Diagonally across the aisle and directly opposite the couple was another vacant berth.

"Shall I take the chance?" Joe wondered.

He decided to run the risk. Standing up, he

pretended to be looking for a window on the opposite side with a better view of the mountains. Without glancing in the direction of the man and woman, he flopped down in the unoccupied seat and began to stare out intently.

"I do not think so," Mr. Fox was mumbling. "Our supplies should last indefinitely as they are."

Joe held his breath, listening with every nerve in his body tense, for the woman's response.

"On the contrary," she said, "our supply line is constantly menaced. We must—ever prepare. No good shall it do us—to be unaware of danger."

"You speak correctly," wheezed the fat man. "It is for us to determine—" His words were drowned out as the train rattled across a bridge. By the time they had passed over, he had returned to his own seat and was reading the newspaper again.

Joe's brain was dancing. "I'm on the trail *this* time for sure," he exulted silently. "Golly, this man and woman have that same stilted way of speaking. But it's clever. I'm sure it wouldn't be noticed by most people, and so never suspected as a way to hide one's nationality."

The ride seemed interminable. At length Mr. Fox and his woman companion disappeared into the buffet car. Joe deemed it wise to stay where he was. From sheer exhaustion, he presently fell asleep. When he awoke, the suspects had not returned.

With a start of dismay Joe bounded to his feet. Had the couple slipped away at some stop? He hurried through the train until he found the conductor.

"No, sir, we haven't stopped anywhere," replied the latter to his query. Just then the train lurched and began to slow down. "Saddler!" the man called loudly.

The train jerked to a stop. In a twinkling the Hardy boy was standing on the platform, straining his eyes under the feeble lights of the tiny depot. Suddenly he saw two familiar figures disembarking. Almost instantly they slipped away in the shadows.

Joe raced toward them around the opposite side of the station. In the gloom he stumbled over a hitching post. Then, a few yards ahead, he saw a pair of powerful headlights stab the darkness in a wide arc as a big automobile backed and turned around.

Flattening himself against the side of the building, Joe waited until Mr. Fox and his companion got in. Then, in the brief instant before the driver could engage the gears, the boy dashed up and climbed, unnoticed, onto the back bumper.

With a roar the auto leaped ahead, the headlights spraying the road. Joe could hear muffled voices above the noise of the wheels.

Carefully bracing himself, he leaned far around one side of the tonneau and held his breath, listening.

There was no mistaking the voice he now could hear plainly. It was that of Fox.

"No, no unusual news," the fat man was saying testily. "How is the Chief?"

There was an inaudible reply from somewhere inside the car.

"That is good," the fat man rumbled again. "And how is the Professor?"

Joe gave a start that almost loosened his grip. Try as he might, however, he could not distinguish the reply.

"No," boomed the fat man, "we have nothing in particular to report this time. Oh, I did receive a telegram. Yes, on the train. It was from Thorn, the cursed fool. Does he not know that sending messages through regular channels is against the rules of our——"

At that instant the automobile hit a terrific bump that sent Joe Hardy crashing into the road.

CHAPTER XVII

FOLLOWED!

STUNNED by the impact, Joe lay motionless for several moments. Gradually the spots dancing before his eyes faded away.

He was about to drag himself to his feet when a bright light suddenly blinded him. There was a sickening screech of brakes and a car slithered to a stop not more than half a dozen feet away.

"Hello! You hurt?" called a worried voice, as a young man hurried over.

"N-no, I think I'm all right," Joe gasped weakly. He stood up with the aid of the newcomer.

"Hit-and-run driver, I s'pose," said the man. "Such fellows should be shot. Come on, I'll take you back to town."

Obligingly the stranger turned his sedan around and sped toward the lights of Saddler. By the time they had reached the outskirts Joe felt better.

"Shall I take you to the hospital?" the fellow asked solicitously.

"A hotel will be all right, thanks," Joe replied.

They pulled up in front of a large, ramshackle building facing the village square. Joe climbed out.

"I certainly owe you a vote of thanks for helping me," he said.

"Forget it," returned the driver breezily. "Glad to 've had the chance. So long!"

With a friendly wave he drove off. Joe tumbled into bed and slept heavily. Considerably refreshed, he awoke early the next morning. Several possible plans of action confronted him. Should he attempt to find out where Fox and his companions had gone?

"That might take me a month, under the circumstances," he mused to himself. "No, I'd better get back to Beegle and see if Frank left any news." Suddenly his face tensed. "First I'll see if I can unearth anything around here about Professor Morse. He was last heard from at Saddler."

After a bath and a hearty breakfast the Hardy lad set out for the sheriff's office.

"Howdy," greeted a bewhiskered fellow whose rusty badge was the only sign of his official standing. "Lookin' for somebody or somethin', are ye?"

"I'd like to see the sheriff, sir."

"Wal, ye be lookin' right at 'im," said the man with a chuckle. "Yep, I be sheriff, and chief and coroner."

Suppressing a smile, Joe took the battered chair the man offered him. "I'm trying to get information about a Professor Morse, who disappeared several years ago somewhere around here," he stated.

The sheriff stroked his whiskers. "Hm, Professor Morse, eh? Be ye sartin that's his handle? Now, they was a feller named Snodgrass used to live around these parts. One day he up and plumb disappeared. Ain't been seen since."

"Was that very long ago?" Joe asked, wondering if this was any clue at all.

"Wal, lemme see. That must've been back in '98."

It was obvious that no help was to be had from Saddler's sheriff. Though the official seemed eager to spend his morning talking, Joe thanked the man for his information and hurried off.

"Now what?" he wondered.

Standing on the village square, he happened to glance toward a small, neat building with a sign *Public Library* dangling over the entrance. On impulse Joe went inside, where a matronly woman was cataloguing books at a desk.

"Good morning, sir," she said pleasantly.

When Joe explained his mission her eyes lighted up. "Professor Morse? The name sounds familiar. Let me think a moment."

She gazed out the window for a few seconds while Joe waited.

"I remember," she exclaimed suddenly. "He

used to come in here, I'm sure. Just a minute."
She hurried to a stack of files and rapidly
thumbed through a mass of indexed records.
"Yes, here is his name and card. The last time
he borrowed a book was several years ago."

Excitedly Joe listened while the librarian described the professor as she remembered him.

"I haven't seen nor heard of him since that
time," she said finally. "I'll be glad to let you
know if I do."

Highly elated over the information, scanty
though it was, Joe thanked the woman and went
out. For a while he strolled back and forth
along the square speculating on his next move.

"Guess I'd better go back to Beegle and get
in touch with Frank or Dad," he decided at
length, and headed for the depot.

An hour elapsed before a train to Beegle arrived. Chafing at the delay, Joe discovered to
his further dismay that it was a local. It was
nearly midnight when, after a bumpy, monotonous ride, he finally got off. To his astonishment and delight Detective Kelly was standing
on the platform.

"For goodness' sake, what are *you* doing
here?" the Hardy lad laughed.

"Wal, I might ask the same o' you, Joe,"
smiled the latter, changing his cigar from one
corner of his mouth to the other. "Don't you
know a good detective always pokes around
stations at crazy hours?"

"I haven't had a good meal since I left,"

said Joe. "Let's eat somewhere. Do you know if Frank carried out his plan?"

They went into an all-night restaurant and ordered steak.

"If I knew where Frank is now I'd be a mind-reader," Kelly chuckled. "Anyhow, let's start at the beginning. Remember that fellow who called on you two just before you left?"

"I certainly do, Kelly. He almost made me miss the *Flying Express*."

"Well, I had a time with him, trying to keep him off your brother's trail when Frank took a plane to Bainville to catch the *Flying Express*."

Joe almost forgot the meat he had been so eager to eat as he listened to the detective unfold his story.

"Anyhow, I managed to steer the fellow away from Frank," Kelly went on with a significant tap on the pocket where he kept a small black-jack.

Joe smiled knowingly. "Then what?" he asked.

"I had a phone call from your Dad."

"You did? That's great! What did he say?"

Kelly grinned. "Seems your Aunt Gertrude tossed a monkey wrench into things."

"As usual," Joe smiled grimly. "What did she do?"

"It seems that when yore Dad was talkin' to Frank on the phone a few days ago——"

"I remember," said Joe eagerly.

"Well, the old lady—excuse me, I mean yore

Aunt Gertrude—comes to the office to bawl your Dad out for lettin' you two gallivant around."

Joe smiled again. "That's nothing unusual."

"While she's waitin' for him to finish talkin' a man comes into the office. Aunt Gertrude thinks he's about to murder your Dad, so she whacks him over the head with her umbrella, *wham!*"

Joe laughed outright. "Who was the fellow?"

"Then your father stops talkin' to Frank and turns around to see what's goin' on. Just as he does that your Aunt grabs the phone and says, 'Fenton, for goodness' sake defend yourself! This man was tryin' to kill you!"

By now Joe was so convulsed with mirth that he could scarcely keep his seat. "If that isn't Aunt Gertrude to a T," he exclaimed as tears of laughter rolled down his cheeks. "I suppose the murderer was just some delivery boy."

Kelly took another mouthful of steak. "He was a perfectly harmless client of your Dad. Name, if I remember, was Court. Andrew Court, I think it was. He just dropped in to see about some legal matter."

"Now we know why Dad suddenly stopped talking on the line that time," said Joe. "Frank thought something had happened to him. Did he have any other message for us?"

"He said he couldn't join you yet, but to keep right on with what you're doing. He's on the track of some of the group of spies who are employed in a munitions factory. He had to wait for that to break.''

''Good enough,'' said Joe, picking up his fork again and diving into his half-cooled steak. Suddenly he glanced at a clock overhead. ''Wonder what has been happening to Frank since he left?''

* * * * *

''I'm glad Kelly got rid of that man,'' Frank thought as he settled down in his seat on the plane.

As the engines roared for the take-off a lean, hawk-nosed man jumped aboard, panting slightly. He dropped into a vacant seat opposite Frank. A moment later the craft swept into the skies.

Frank sat musing to himself. Suddenly he thought he felt the eyes of the new passenger fastened on him. Boldly the boy turned and looked squarely at the fellow who quickly averted his gaze.

''Wonder who *he* is?'' Frank asked himself. As the ship droned onward he caught the man staring at him repeatedly. ''Either he's on *my* trail or I should be on *his*,'' the Hardy lad decided at length.

He resolved to pay no further attention to the annoying stranger until they should land. Finally the muffled thunder of the engines died away and the great machine glided downward.

''Bainville,'' announced the hostess as they

came to a stop. "Ten minutes' rest for those who are going on."

Frank hastily disembarked and went into the administration building without a glance behind. A few moments later he was seated in the airport car with several other passengers. The hawk-nosed man, to Frank's relief, apparently had remained aboard the air liner.

Then to his dismay the fellow rushed up just as they were starting. This time he managed to find a seat directly behind Frank. The boy thought fast. He had twenty minutes in which to catch the *Flying Express*. The ride to town would take ten. In the remaining ten he would have to elude his pursuer, get to the depot, buy his ticket . . .

"Grand Hotel," announced the driver as he swung the big car alongside the curb in front of a large building on the main street.

Frank jumped out and began walking rapidly. His worst fears were realized when he turned a corner. As he did so, he saw the hawk-nosed man not far behind.

A thought suddenly flashed through the boy's brain. He turned abruptly and went into a fashionable-looking restaurant, seating himself near the back of the room. As he had expected, the man strolled past and looked through the window, then stood on the curb pretending to watch the flow of traffic.

"I'll fix *you*," Frank muttered grimly. He summoned a waiter.

"Yes, sir. Will you order dinner, sir?" the man asked.

"I've heard a lot about your good cooking here," Frank said truthfully. "I wonder if I might see your kitchen."

"Certainly you may," agreed the waiter, radiating pleasure. "The chef will be glad to show you around."

Frank lost no time, for his watch revealed that the remaining minutes were few. One look inside the kitchen told him where the back door was. Before the astonished employees could make a move he had disappeared outside.

As luck would have it, a policeman was standing on a near-by corner.

"Which way is the station, sir?" Frank asked hurriedly.

"Right there, son," replied the officer, pointing.

To Frank's delight the depot was just across the street. In thirty seconds he was standing before the ticket window.

"Better hurry," said the agent, handing a ticket to the lad. "The *Flying Express* is in. She'll be leaving right away."

The Hardy boy turned away. With a chill of alarm he saw the hawk-nosed man hurrying through the doorway toward him.

CHAPTER XVIII

AN ACCIDENT

For a split second Frank stood rooted to the spot. Then he realized the hawk-nosed man had not seen him. Pulling his hat brim down over his eyes, the boy made a dash for the tracks. Running alongside the train, he barely managed to seize the hand railing of the observation platform at the rear. In the nick of time he swung aboard.

"Whew! That was a close one," he said to himself.

Straightening his clothes, he jerked open the door and entered the last car. He peered out a window.

"I don't see that fellow anywhere. I hope he missed the train!"

Temporarily relieved that his pursuer had failed to catch him, Frank sat down in the nearest seat to get his breath. Then he reached into an inside pocket and drew out a neatly typed envelope addressed to Mr. J. T. Thorn, just as a porter came along the aisle.

"I have a telegram here. Would you mind delivering it?" the Hardy boy asked the attendant.

"Telegram? Yes, Ah surely will, suh. You know the gentleman, suh?"

"No, I don't. I was asked to bring it on the train."

The fellow smiled and took the envelope. Frank thought it best not to follow at the moment.

To the boy's dismay the porter returned, still holding the message.

"I'se awful sorry, suh, but dey's nobody by dat name on de train."

When the man had left, the lad sat glumly looking out the window. Suddenly the colored fellow reappeared.

"Pardon me, suh, but dey's a man up in de nex' car says he's Mr. Thorn."

Frank looked at the porter incredulously. "Really?"

"Yes, suh. Says he cain't hear very good, but one of de other passengers told him dey's a telegram for a Mr. Thorn. He be in de second seat from de front of de nex' car, suh. Sittin' by hisself." The man hesitated for a moment and peered around. "Dey's sumpin' funny 'bout him, suh. He done say he's deaf, but when Ah talk to him he hear everything Ah say!"

Frank presently left his seat and went into the next car, where he stopped in front of the water cooler and poured himself a drink. Out of the corner of his eye he could see in the place mentioned by the porter a thin, surly-looking individual wearing thick spectacles.

"So that's Mr. Thorn," Frank mused.

The man was intently scanning a document of some sort. Frank watched him for a moment, then slipped into a vacant seat near by. After an uneventful ride the train finally began to slow down.

"Saddler! Saddler!" shouted the conductor.

"He'll get off here, I'll bet my shirt," Frank said to himself.

Tingling with anticipation he waited as the *Flying Express* came to a stop. Sure enough, Mr. Thorn hurried off the train, with Frank following at a discreet distance. Crossing the platform, the suspect disappeared inside the station where the boy could see him writing a telegram.

The Hardy lad watched him through the glass-paneled door. The man blotted what he had written and handed the sheet to a clerk. As the man turned away Frank hurried inside.

Casually he picked up the blotter Thorn had used and scanned its surface. To his delight a message was plainly legible, although, of course, it was backwards. Eagerly the boy spelled it out, then hurried into the seclusion of a phone booth. Drawing out paper and pencil, he jotted down what he had seen before he might forget it. Then he read the message over:

M. B. WAXEN EN ROUTE FLYING
EXPRESS LEAVING THURSDAY. YOUR WIRE
RECEIVED. IF MISTAKE WIRE HOME AT
ONCE. THORN.

Hastily stuffing the sheet into his pocket, Frank dashed outside. The man he was following was nowhere to be seen.

"Never mind, this is more important just now," Frank said to himself, bringing out his copy of Thorn's telegram again. "Waxen is on the next *Flying Express*. When those two men get together they'll realize that somebody sent a fake message."

"And what's more," he told himself, "if Joe's telegram got to Mr. Fox, and if Fox meets Thorn and Waxen, they'll be all the more certain that somebody is on their trail!"

He knitted his brow and thought hard for a moment. "There's one thing certain. I must warn Joe not to deliver the next message!"

Frank went immediately to a phone and called the rooming house at Beegle. The owner said the younger Hardy lad had not been in for some time.

"Guess I'll have to go back there myself and find him!" Frank burst out impatiently.

Once more he met an obstacle. There was no train for Beegle that would get him there in time. Suddenly his eye caught sight of a large moving van just outside the window of the station. Hurrying from the waiting room he went up to the driver and put a question to him.

"Beegle? Sure, we're goin' right through there. Want to ride all night? This is a slow contraption."

Frank nodded, whereupon the man motioned him into the seat beside himself. After what seemed an eternity they reached the outskirts of town and then commenced a slow, monotonous journey through the countryside. Despite the stranger's efforts to carry on a friendly conversation, Frank was quiet, his impatience mounting. But he could do nothing.

"Well, how 'bout a hamburger?" yawned the mover as they pulled into a little town.

The big truck rumbled to a stop while Frank bit his nails at the delay. Suddenly he thought he recognized a figure just entering a parked sedan near by.

"Thorn!" flashed through his head, but before he could follow his impulse to race after the man the car roared off.

"What's the trouble? Seein' ghosts?" queried the truck driver as Frank stood staring after the vanishing auto.

The boy laughed grimly and followed his companion into the restaurant. By the time they were ready to start again the Hardy lad was seething with impatience. Half an hour later the driver suddenly slowed up and squinted ahead.

"Hmph. Looks like the bridge ain't there."

Sure enough, a small wooden structure just ahead evidently had been torn loose by a rainstorm. In the glare of the headlights a crudely lettered sign hanging on one of the posts spelled

Detour and pointed toward a rutted country road.

"If that ain't the limit," cursed the mover, pulling at the steering wheel.

Frank, almost beside himself with dismay, said nothing. The big truck bounced and lurched along, nearly throwing its passengers from the seat. Suddenly the man uttered a yell and gave the wheel a desperate yank. It was too late. The heavy front part of the van slipped in the treacherous mud and came to rest in a ditch with a broken axle.

"There ain't nothin' to do but find a phone and git a wrecker," observed the driver disgustedly. "And nobody'll come out here till morning, I'm sure of that."

"I'll find a house if there's one to be found," offered Frank, his spirits dropping still lower.

The Hardy boy set out at a rapid pace. It was now too late for him to get to Joe, he decided, but a telephone call still might save the day. He would take the risk of being overheard. For a good twenty minutes he walked steadily. Suddenly he saw a farm cottage. Would there be a phone in it?

He almost cried out for joy when the owner answered in the affirmative. Yet another disappointment awaited him. The telephone exchange was closed for the night!

After a fitful sleep at the kindly man's home, Frank and the truckman arose. Hours were consumed in fixing the van and in trying to reach the younger Hardy lad. After several attempts Frank finally heard the voice of the woman who owned the rooming house in Beegle.

"Joe Hardy? Sorry, he's left."

With sinking heart Frank hung up. His plans for catching his brother now were utterly hopeless. What would happen to Joe? Would he be captured? Frank shuddered at the thought.

As he walked back toward the van he was startled by the roar of an engine. Looking upward, he saw a trim, fast little airplane swoop down and land in a pasture, just behind a barn.

"By golly," he exclaimed to himself, "maybe there's a chance——"

He set off on a run and reached the ship just as its owner, a gangling, pleasant-faced youth, stepped out.

"Howdy, stranger," greeted the latter.

"Could you by any chance fly me to Bainville?" Frank asked, trying to control his excitement.

"Bainville? Sure I could—later," drawled the aviator. "Got to take my girl for a ride now. Promised her I would. Here she comes."

Frank's heart sank. A beautiful girl was hurrying toward them from the farmhouse.

"Oh, hello," she said when she saw the Hardy boy.

"This fella wants me to fly him to Bainville, Martha," the young pilot explained, "but I told him we had a date."

Despite his feelings of impatience, Frank

smiled at the girl, who returned it. "I'm sorry," he apologized, "I shouldn't want to interfere with any plans——"

Martha laughed gaily. "Don't worry about me, Jimmy. You just go ahead and take this young man to Bainville. He seems very nice," she added coyly.

Frank felt himself reddening, at which both the others laughed outright.

"Say," chuckled the pilot, "before you two get any friendlier I guess I'd *better* fly this fellow to Bainville!"

Frank's heart leaped. His watch told him that he had an excellent chance of catching Joe through this unexpected opportunity. Quickly forgetting his embarrassment he thanked the girl for giving up her ride and hopped into the tiny ship.

"Just a couple of minutes," called Jimmy. "Got to get some more gas." He set out for the farmhouse at a trot.

"Do you suppose he will be away long?" Frank asked the young woman anxiously.

He consulted his watch for the tenth time in as many minutes. His safety margin was rapidly diminishing. Finally, when he thought he would burst with impatience, Jimmy reappeared carrying two large tins of gasoline.

"Let me help you," Frank offered eagerly.

Together the boys emptied the fluid into the tank and prepared the ship for the take-off.

"How long a ride is it to Bainville?" Frank queried.

"Depends on the wind up above."

"I want to catch a certain train. I hope we can make it."

The pilot's reply was lost in the roar of the engine as they sped across the rough ground and shot upward over a fringe of tall trees.

CHAPTER XIX

High above the pasture the little plane levelled off as Jimmy set his course.

"Good weather for flying," he shouted above the hammering of the motor.

"Great!" replied Frank. "Nice little ship, too."

"Like to try the controls?"

As Frank nodded Jimmy attached the dual control stick and rudder and motioned to the Hardy boy to take hold. He noted with surprise the ease of handling the plane, which practically flew by itself.

"I think we'll go up another thousand feet," the pilot said. "Better tail wind there."

Following the fellow's instructions Frank gently nosed the plane upward and began a slow climb. As the altimeter registered eight thousand feet he levelled off. Jimmy pointed to a large factory directly below them, then indicated his wrist watch.

"That's Henryville. We're making better than a hundred and twenty miles an hour."

The Hardy boy grinned. There was a chance to intercept Joe, after all! He steadied the plane as it hit a series of bumps.

158

"You're a born flyer, Frank," his companion burst out enthusiastically. "Why don't you get a plane yourself?"

"Too busy chasing sp—" Frank checked himself. "Too busy," he finished.

Despite his anxiety lest he miss Joe at the Bainville depot Frank was enjoying himself thoroughly. For a while the two young men flew without speaking. Then Jimmy tapped his passenger's arm and pointed downward.

"Beegle! We're ahead of schedule."

"Thank goodness," Frank breathed, praying that their good fortune would continue.

The Hardy boy had been scanning the landscape eagerly, wondering if he could spot the spy camp. He saw nothing that looked like such a place.

"All right, Frank, I'll take over," Jimmy shouted presently. "There's the Bainville airport."

The pilot, shutting off the power, began circling downward. Then, gunning the motor in spurts to keep up flying speed he brought the ship to a perfect three-point landing. A glance at his watch told Frank that he had only ten minutes to get to the railroad station.

Thanking the flyer profusely and promising to get in touch with him later, he hurried inside the administration building, half hoping that Joe might have arrived shortly before on his way to catch the *Flying Express*. His brother was not there.

"Air liner from Beegle was in and just left," an official told Frank. "Yes, I believe there was a young fellow answering your description aboard. He probably went to town in the airport bus with the other passengers."

Unfortunately there was no vehicle around at the moment, inasmuch as no more air liners were due for several hours. Biting his lips in desperation, Frank strode up and down, wondering how to reach the *Flying Express* in time. Just then a motorcycle roared up and a casual young fellow got off. On impulse Frank ran up to him.

"May I ask a great favor of you?"

"Sure."

"I have to catch a train that leaves in less than ten minutes. Could you take me to it?"

"Don't see why not, long's you don't mind bouncin' around a little." The lad pointed to the second saddle over the rear fender. "Just hop aboard and hold onto me."

Off they roared in a swirl of dust. For the first few seconds it was all Frank could do to catch his breath and hold on at the same time. Suddenly they hit a terrific bump. The Hardy boy bounced a foot from the saddle and came down with a jar that made his teeth rattle.

"If only Joe could see me now," he smiled grimly as soon as he had caught his grip again.

Little did Frank know that his brother was saying those exact words at that very instant, nearly two miles away at the Bainville depot.

"Oh, never mind," an old lady with a market basket was cackling. "I'll count the penny lost. It will teach me not to chew so much gum."

"I think it will drop now, Madam," grunted Joe, whose face was red in his effort to loosen a coin stuck in a chewing gum slot machine.

He gave the metal a smart rap and the cent suddenly rolled out, tinkling against the stone platform.

"Just a minute, there," barked an authoritative voice, and a burly officer of the law stepped up, grabbing Joe's sleeve. "Just what do you think yore doin'?"

Joe looked nonplussed. "Why, I—I was trying to get the——"

"Oh, you were? Tryin' to rob slot machines, eh? Well, you'll just come along and see the sheriff."

"Please," Joe protested in growing dismay, as a muffled train whistle sounded in the distance, "I was trying to get back this lady's money. She put it in and didn't get any gum out."

"That is absolutely right," spoke up the old lady. "Now you just let that boy alone, Deputy. He isn't trying to rob any more than *you*."

"Oh, is that so?" The officer looked at Joe and the woman hesitantly. "All that bangin' and rattlin' just to get back a penny, eh?"

The old lady shook a bony forefinger in the man's face. "Listen here, didn't your mother teach you to save your pennies? Very well,

that's just what I have always done. When I
put a penny in a machine and get nothing out, I
do something about it. Thanks to this boy here,
I have my coin back!"

The old lady's defiant tirade and her stern
look had their desired effect. The officer flushed
scarlet and walked away. Before Joe could so
much as thank the old woman, there was a rumble and a screech of brakes as the great *Flying
Express* slowed to a stop alongside the platform.

"All aboard!"

Joe was halfway up the steps when he heard
a sound that made him whirl around in surprise.
It was a familiar whistle, repeated three times.

"Don't block the entrance," said the conductor, eyeing Joe sharply.

The Hardy lad jumped back to the platform
and gazed about. Suddenly he saw a familiar
figure astride a motorcycle which had just
slithered to a stop in the parking area.

"Frank!" squealed Joe, his eyes popping in
astonishment.

Leaping from the motorcycle, the older
brother dashed along the platform, almost col-
liding with Joe in his haste. There was a loud
clang as the train started up jerkily.

"Are we getting on, or aren't we?" Joe asked
tensely.

Frank's answer was to leap for the lowest
step of the car in front of them. "Come on!"

A moment later the two were seated com-
fortably inside one of the sleepers.

"Golly, I wasn't sure I'd make it," Frank panted, mopping his face. "I've had plenty of humdinging rides in my life, but *that* one on the motorcycle beats them all!"

"Suppose you tell me what this is all about," Joe suggested, smiling at his brother's disheveled appearance.

Frank's face took on a grim look. "Where are your telegrams? The ones we faked?"

"Right here in my pocket. I was just going to have the porter page Mr. Waxen. He's the one who's supposed to be aboard today."

Frank nodded. "I know. But we're not going to give it to him, or to any of the others. We'll have to tear them up."

"Tear them up? Why, Frank, your scheme worked! I found Fox the first day! And now——"

"They're going to suspect us any minute, Joe." The older boy then related his experience of the previous day. "You see, Joe? As soon as Waxen catches up with Thorn and Fox they'll all know the telegrams were hoaxes."

Joe whistled in surprise. "What do you know about that? Wish we could locate that spy Waxen, though."

"I've an idea that we can try right now. Find some luggage marked with his initials, M. B. W."

"Maybe he hasn't any baggage with him. Let's try it, anyhow."

Pretending merely to be stretching their legs

the boys strolled through the train, but there was no sign of suitcases marked with M. B. W.

"Guess your idea's no good, Frank. We'll have to figure out something else."

"I know! How about starting a few conversations? Maybe we'll meet some fellows who speak in that stilted sort of way."

Joe scratched his head dubiously. "All right, I'm game. First we'd better think up a few things to say."

"Oh, anything will do," snorted Frank. "Come on, let's start with that sissy-looking fellow over there."

Together they strolled up to a thin, browbeaten man. Frank smiled at him. "Stuffy in here, isn't it?" he remarked pleasantly.

"Oh, deucedly," chattered the other, sniffing at a handkerchief. "I find smelling salts excellent under the circumstances. Would you care to borrow mine?"

"No, thanks," Frank replied, suppressing a laugh. Winking at Joe, he moved onward and stopped beside a heavy-set, uncouth-looking fellow. "Bumpy ride, isn't it?" the lad observed casually.

"Yeah. So what?" challenged the man with a scowl.

Frank motioned to Joe and they went into the car ahead. "So far, so bad," he whispered.

"How about that one?" Joe nodded toward a small, middle-aged man whose chin ran down thickly into his neck.

They approached him. "Good afternoon, sir," Frank greeted him pleasantly.

"Dear me, what's good about it?" asked the stranger with a worried frown. "Young man, what do you think my wife is going to say when I get home? I was supposed to g-get home yesterday but business detained me. She doesn't like me to be late."

Frank laughed. "Oh, she probably won't mind. Maybe you should have brought her a present."

"A present? *A present?* Young man, I wish I had the money I've spent on presents for my wife. In those packages there I have a new book, a pair of gloves and some silk stockings and—and——"

Half convulsed with mirth the boys managed to restrain themselves long enough to sympathize with the man for a few moments. Then Frank nudged his brother and walked up to the front of the sleeper, where a swarthy-faced traveler with beady eyes sat watching their approach.

"Pardon me, sir, but could I borrow a match?" Frank asked politely.

The man surveyed him deliberately. "Are there not—proper authorities whose function it is—to dispense matches?" he inquired with an air of stilted formality.

Frank smiled with pretended sheepishness. "I'm sorry, sir."

The boy shot his brother a significant look, as

the two went back through the car and into the next one.

"That's our man, I'll bet a million," Frank exclaimed softly as they resumed their seats.

Joe nodded tensely. "I think you're right! If that's the case we'd better——"

At that instant there came a terrific jolt, then a crash that hurled both boys over the back of the seat ahead of them and out into the aisle. At once a chorus of hideous screams sounded on all sides!

CHAPTER XX

"FRANK! Where are you?"

Dazed and shaken, Joe found himself tightly wedged beneath a seat. Where his brother might be, he could only guess. He called again above the hubbub about him. There was no response.

Joe shuddered as he listened to the shouts and groans of the victims around him. Then, wincing with pain, he began the task of struggling free. It was difficult. One foot was jammed beneath an iron bar, the other lay in a heap of jagged glass, and both arms were pinned beneath debris.

Suddenly his left foot came free. Next he managed to pull his left arm out. Then began a long struggle to wriggle from beneath the seat. Finally, his strength almost exhausted, he managed to get up.

"Frank!"

The motionless figure of his brother was the first thing he spotted. The boy was sprawled across the aisle with blood oozing from a gash in his scalp. Frantically Joe felt his brother's pulse. Although weak, it was beating regularly.

167

"Frank! Wake up!"

Joe gazed about him for the first time. Everywhere, lying in heaps, were other passengers. Many were beyond aid. Others groaned and cried piteously.

Suddenly the boy noticed a familiar face. It was swarthy. The pudgy lips were moving soundlessly. The man's eyes were closed.

"Waxen!" the thought flashed to Joe.

He took another look at Frank, who appeared to be coming to. Then he laid his brother's head gently back on the floor and crawled to where the suspect was lying, just inside the splintered entrance to the car. With a start the lad realized that the fellow must have been thrown there from the platform. As Joe approached he could hear faint mumbling.

"Mus' destroy babers, mus' destroy—" The voice trailed off. Joe watched the distorted face tensely. The mouth opened again. "Babers—no, pa—pers! Mus' get to—to gamp, no—ca—mp. Beegul! Bu—gul!"

Then followed a torrent of words in some language which Joe could not make out. Finally the man gasped and fell silent.

Satisfied from the fellow's breathing that he was not seriously injured, Joe slowly made his way back to Frank. To his joy the older Hardy boy was sitting up.

"Wh—where am I? Wh—what happened?"

"Train wreck. How do you feel? You had a bad knock on the head."

"You're telling me!" Frank muttered weakly. Then he managed to smile. "I—I guess I'll be all right now. Boy, does my head ache!"

"Think you can follow me out?" Joe asked.

"Yes. Oh, listen to the screams! We'd better help the injured."

The older boy rapidly recovered himself and the two Hardys set themselves to the task of dragging the injured from the *Flying Express.* One by one, with the assistance of those who had escaped, they laid the victims on the grass and gave what first aid they could. On their fourth trip back into the car Joe stumbled over a heavy-set figure lying across the aisle.

"Let me out of here," wailed a voice. "Will some—person help me or must I—fend for myself?"

Joe turned his head. "It's Waxen," he whispered to Frank, who was just behind him.

"Is he hurt?"

"Not badly, I believe."

He reached out and grabbed the man's arm, pulling him through the tangled mass into the open.

"Very well, that will do," said Waxen petulantly. "I am quite capable of—caring for myself."

"That's gratitude for you," Frank remarked dryly to his brother, as the boys promptly went back into the car to bring out the last victims. "Let's get some water from that creek over there," he suggested a few moments later.

"What do you suppose caused the wreck?" queried Joe as they walked to the stream.

"We'll know pretty soon," responded his brother.

"Help coming!" one of the trainmen bellowed.

A large touring car could be seen bouncing across the fields, raising a cloud of dust behind it. The auto slithered to a stop. A burly man stepped out and looked over the scene.

"How many can you take, Mister?" the chief conductor asked.

"Eight, if they can sit up. Three if they cain't," returned the other. "But they'll be a few more cars comin'. All I could round up at the ranches near mine."

"You better take three of the worst hurt," said the conductor.

He nodded to Frank and Joe, pointing toward three badly injured passengers, whom they might help carry.

"How about me?" whined a voice just then.

The brothers turned to see Waxen sitting alongside the tracks a few yards distant.

"Wait a minute," said the conductor to Frank. He hurried over and passed his hands deftly over the man's body. "You're not hurt, sir."

"But I must get to—town," Waxen said persistently. "I *am* hurt. Most—dangerously. Kindly have me put in that—auto immediately."

"I'm sorry, but we'll have to take care of the injured ones first," said the trainman sternly.

Leaving Waxen scrowling he signalled the Hardys to proceed. Quickly the boys helped to carry the three injured passengers to the auto and carefully propped them inside. The car put about and raced off.

"We have a fellow who's bleeding pretty badly up there in the first coach," the conductor said to Frank, who had shown adeptness at first aid. "Come up and see what you can do."

By the time the lad returned to his brother he found him standing alongside Waxen. The man was talking excitedly.

"Maybe you can help this gentleman out," Joe remarked with a wink at Frank. "He wants to know where we are and how he can get to the nearest town."

"Let us not—quibble," Waxen broke in. "I am interested in—obtaining information concerning the—surrounding countryside, and likewise the location of—the nearest village." His stilted, hesitant speech sounded especially queer amid his surroundings.

"Well," said Frank, "I'm afraid I can't help you very much beyond the fact that we certainly aren't very far from Beegle."

Watching the man's face closely he thought he saw a momentary expression of interest at mention of the town. But Waxen gave no further hint.

"Beegle?" he repeated. "What is that? A

kind of—dog?'' He grunted thickly, then pulled himself laboriously to his feet. ''Agh! Another—limousine arrives. Perhaps I may be so fortunate as to—rent it for the continuation of —my journey.''

The boys watched him as he waddled off. ''If you ask me,'' said Joe, ''he knows more about where he is than he wants us to believe.''

''I was thinking the same thing,'' Frank remarked thoughtfully. ''Did you notice his expression when I mentioned Beegle?''

''I did, and that reminds me—'' Joe went on to tell about the strange phrases the man had uttered inside the car, while Frank had been unconscious.

''Jumping tomcats, Joe, that's the best clue we've had yet,'' the older boy exclaimed when his brother had finished. ''I'll bet that spy camp we're after is right around *here.*''

''I shouldn't be surprised, Frank. Mus'. be nearer Beegle than any other place.''

''Look.'' Frank caught his brother's sleeve. ''He can't get a ride.''

They could see Waxen arguing with both the conductor and the driver of the car that had just arrived. It was apparent that the man was making no headway, for presently he walked off.

''He's leaving!'' Joe exclaimed.

''Then we're going after him,'' Frank whispered.

Waxen, battered suitcase in hand, was stalking off across a large field at the far end of which was a thick forest.

"He'll see us," objected Joe. "We can't follow him across the field."

"We'll wait till he goes into the woods. It rained this morning. Won't be hard to follow his tracks."

Excitedly the boys watched the retreating figure until it was a mere speck in the distance.

"All right, let's start," urged Frank.

Soon they reached the woods. Skirting the outermost fringe of trees they backtracked to the point where Waxen had disappeared.

"There's a footprint," Joe whispered.

"He went this way."

Stealthily the Hardys crept along what appeared to be a well-trod path.

"Do you suppose he knew this trail was here?" Frank speculated with a significant look at Joe.

The latter muttered, "Shouldn't be surprised. This probably goes straight to the spy camp." He smiled happily.

For fifteen minutes they followed Waxen's deeply-imprinted footsteps along the winding path.

"Glad he's a heavy fellow, Frank. Makes our job twice as——"

Crack! The silent air was shattered by a sudden shot. The boys stopped short in their tracks.

"Did somebody shoot him, or did he shoot

somebody else?'' Joe cried after a moment.

He and Frank stood listening for several moments, but nothing more could be heard. Then, tingling with anticipation, they moved on cautiously. Ahead was a bend. Both boys expected to see something of importance around the curve, nor were they disappointed.

"What is it?" Joe asked as they stood half-concealed behind a large tree trunk.

"Looks like the body of a mountain lion. I know. It's a cougar!"

Seeing no sign of anyone about, they stole up to the huge carcass which lay alongside the path. A tiny trickle of blood on one side of the beast's head marked the spot where a bullet had penetrated.

"Hmph. So Waxen carries a pistol," Frank observed.

"Chalk up more evidence against him," said Joe. "People don't carry guns without a reason."

"Well, here are his footprints, same as usual," Frank observed, pointing at the ground. "And there they go, off that way."

As the boys walked on, the gloom of the forest gradually lightened.

"We'll be out in the open any minute, Frank," said Joe.

"Yes, and we'd better go slow from now on. No telling what's ahead."

A few moments later they could see the end of the woods. Creeping from tree to tree they suddenly found themselves facing a broad area covered with tall, waving grass.

"Look, Frank! There he goes!"

A familiar figure could be seen streaking across the far end of the field. Joe squinted against the light.

"There's a house, Frank! Behind that clump of foliage! Jumping tomcats, it's the Rangle ranch!"

There was a low groan, followed by a thud. Joe whirled around to see his brother suddenly slump senseless to the ground.

CHAPTER XXI

THE CARVED SYMBOL

QUICKLY Joe knelt beside the still figure. Frank's forehead was cold and clammy, and his pulse was weak. The younger lad ran back along the path to a small brook they had crossed, soaked his handkerchief in the cool water, and returned quickly.

After several moments of bathing his brother's face, Joe saw the color begin to return. Then Frank's eyelids fluttered open.

"I'm a fine one," he gasped with a faint smile.

"Never mind, just take it easy," Joe advised. "You'll feel better when you get some food."

Out of the corner of one eye he still was watching the broad field in front of them and the ranch house in the distance. Waxen was not to be seen. Just then there was a drone overhead.

"A plane," announced Joe, "and flying low. Gee, something has been thrown out of it!" he added excitedly.

Frank got to his feet. "Do you think it was dropped on purpose?" he asked.

Suddenly his knees crumpled and he sank down again. Joe tried to attend to his brother and at the same time see if anyone might pick up the parcel. In a moment a man whom the boy did not recognize came from the homestead to get the package.

"Golly, I'll bet it *was* dropped on purpose," Joe said with thumping heart. "Maybe it was a bundle of newspapers with underlined messages from the East. I'd certainly like to find out, but we wouldn't dare do anything till later. Suppose you rest in the meantime."

Without protest Frank stretched himself out on the soft ground and almost immediately fell asleep. Joe went in search of blueberries and other food which the forest afforded. By the time he got back it was dark.

"Still asleep?" he whispered.

His brother's heavy, regular breathing gave him his answer.

"He'll be safe here," Joe decided. "I think I'll do a little scouting around alone."

He set out across the field. As he drew closer to the ranch house he was disappointed to see no light in it.

"Maybe it's a trap. I'd better watch my step."

Stealthily he approached the gloomy structure and its cluster of outbuildings, pausing every few seconds to listen. There was not a sound except the gentle sighing of the wind. Joe suppressed a shudder at the loneliness of the place.

"The coast seems to be clear," he decided. "I'll have a look in some of the windows."

Stealing up he peered inside. As he had feared, he could see nothing. Finally, with a brief look around the darkened grounds, he turned and made his way back through the tall grass to the woods.

"Frank, where are you?"

"Right over here," came the reassuring reply as his brother emerged through the gloom. "I was just wondering where you'd gone."

The younger Hardy lad related what he had done. "There's nothing more we can do until morning," he said. "Let's eat this food, get a good sleep and be ready for whatever happens."

They awoke to a dull, cloudy day, feeling much refreshed. Just as Joe was about to start off for more blueberries Frank uttered a low exclamation.

"Listen!"

A muffled sound like that of a distant motor could be heard. "It's coming from Rangle's," Joe exclaimed. "Wait, I'll find out for certain."

In the twinkling of an eye he had swung himself into a tall oak tree near by. For a few seconds he grunted and thrashed around among the branches, then——

"This is great, Frank. Aha, there's the truck! Right alongside the ranch house."

"Is it moving? Can you see anybody?" Frank called, fairly bursting with excitement.

"Two men are getting into it. One of them looks like Pete. Can't see the other very well. Wait a minute, now I can! It's Waxen, Frank, I'm sure!"

The sounds suddenly became louder.

"They're starting off," came his brother's voice from the top of the tree. "They're heading this way!"

"Good! Maybe they're going to the spy camp," Frank added. "What luck for us if they are!"

There was a long interval of silence from Joe. Frank paced up and down impatiently, listening to the growing roar of the motor.

"Shucks, they're turning off, Frank. But they're not far away. They're running on what looks like an old wagon track."

"Where are they heading? Into the woods?"

No answer. Then, "Yes. About a quarter of a mile from us. There they go. Gee, I can't see them any more."

"Come on down. We'll go after them."

No sooner had Joe dropped to the ground when the noise of the engine ceased abruptly.

"That's good," said Frank. "They must have parked."

Without further hesitation the boys plunged through the thick of the forest in the direction Joe pointed out. For nearly an hour they floundered about in the dense tangle without seeing a sign either of the wagon road or the machine.

Suddenly Frank seized his brother's sleeve. "Look through there, past that big tree. Isn't that some metal shining?"

"It's the truck, Frank," Joe whispered hoarsely, making a lunge toward the object.

"Careful. Somebody might see us."

Restraining themselves with difficulty the brothers crept as softly as possible through the underbrush. Suddenly they found themselves on the rutted trail. Not ten feet from where they stepped out was a large truck.

"That's the one, Frank," Joe whispered.

For several moments the Hardys peered about and listened intently. Apparently Waxen and the rancher were nowhere in the vicinity.

"Where do you suppose they went?" asked Joe.

Frank was examining something on the bark of a near-by birch. "Come here, Joe. Look at this."

"A carving of a bugle! What do you suppose that means?"

As they stood staring at a perfectly designed bugle carved in the wood, Frank thought it looked strange. "It's backward from the way one usually sees it in pictures," he said with a puzzled frown. "I wonder if that means anything."

"It might be a signal of some sort," mused Joe. Suddenly his eyes popped and he clapped his brother on the shoulder. "Frank! Remember what I told you about those queer phrases and words Waxen was muttering right after the wreck?"

"Yes. I——"

"One of them sounded like 'bugle.' Really it did, Frank! At first I thought he was saying 'Beegle.' Maybe he was saying *both*."

Frank knitted his brow. "Bugle . . . Bugle . . . Beegle . . ." he repeated to himself as if to test the sound of the words. "I wonder if we could figure out any connection there, Joe."

For a while both boys were silent. Then Joe uttered a whoop. "I have it! The *bugle* is some sort of a symbol used by the spies."

Frank stared wide-eyed at his brother. "I think you've hit it! The carving must be a trail mark! Let's see if we can find another."

Scarcely able to control their excitement they scoured the vicinity, carefully studying every tree. Presently Frank gave a cry of triumph. "Here it is! Right on this old oak!"

Joe hurried up and peered at the picture in the bark. "This one points in the *other* direction! Yes, we're on the trail now, sure as you're alive."

"In that case the third mark won't be far off," stated his brother. "Come on, let's have a look."

Although there seemed to be no actual road between the strange signs the boys, by following the direction in which the bugle mouthpieces pointed, rapidly located a dozen more. An hour later they had come a long distance but apparently were not yet at the end of the trail.

Suddenly Joe stopped. "There's something that looks like a fence, Frank!"

"It *is* a fence. Made of saplings."

They had come out into a small clearing. A few feet from where they stood was a solid wall made of narrow young trees at least twelve feet high. It ran as far as they could see in either direction.

The brothers were about to inspect the barricade more closely when they heard the sound of voices. Instantly they sank out of sight in the underbrush. At the same time a head appeared over the top of the palings, directly in front of them.

"That's Pete, the rancher," Joe whispered in his brother's ear.

As the Hardys watched intently, the huge form of the man reached the top of the fence. Quickly he drew up a ladder from behind him and set it down on the outside. When he had climbed to the ground he tossed the ladder back over the rim of the saplings and disappeared in the woods.

Joe clutched his brother. "We must get inside that place right away!"

Frank shook his head. "We'd better wait till dark. If it's really the place Dad asked us to find, it is a dangerous one!"

CHAPTER XXII

A BIG DISCOVERY

"Let's climb trees and have a look at what's inside that mysterious fence," suggested Frank.

From the tops of two oaks the boys saw a cluster of large, low buildings far inside what seemed to be miles of sapling fence. After a good look they scrambled down to compare notes.

"We're really on the track of something *this* time," Frank rejoiced. "Let's make a vine ladder. As soon as it's dark we'll scoot over the top on it."

The work of constructing one strong enough to hold their weight took them several hours, for they took turns finding the proper strands and locating some food. Just as they were completing their task they heard a rustling sound behind them. A low, menacing growl came from the underbrush not ten feet away.

Instinctively both boys held their breaths. Suddenly the snout of a huge bear poked itself out at them. A pair of cruel, bleary eyes riveted the lads to the spot as the enormous animal lumbered toward them.

"He's a grizzly and he looks hungry!" Frank whispered hoarsely.

With his eye Joe measured the distance between the fence and himself, and between the bear and himself.

"It's going to be a close shave," he whispered. "But it's either the fence or the bear!"

Together the boys raced to the wall, carrying their ladder between them. Standing a few feet from the barricade, Frank hurled the vines high into the air. Uncurling like a snake, they fell neatly over the rim of the saplings.

"Go ahead!" he ordered tensely.

Quickly the younger brother scrambled up, crouched for a moment on top the wall, then dropped soundlessly inside. Breathlessly Frank waited for a tug on the vine, for the bear had nearly reached him. When the pull came he scooted up the ladder just in time.

"We'd better not stay here," advised Joe. "That looks like a main entrance to that building over there," he added, pointing.

"You're right. How about our hiding in the shed over there?"

Quickly the brothers walked to it and pushed open the door. No one was inside, so the boys hustled out of sight.

"There's nothing much here," Joe remarked when their eyes became accustomed to the darkness.

"Yes, there is," contradicted Frank excitedly as he yanked open a trap door in the floor. "Rifles!"

Dimly they could see a long line of gun barrels

stacked tightly in a small cellar. Further investigation showed nothing else of interest in the shed, but the boys deemed it best to wait until darkness should fall before venturing outside. As luck would have it, the rain which had threatened all day began to fall. Heavy clouds turned day into night. Frank rose and looked out.

"I think it's dark enough now, Joe. Let's get started."

Ahead, among the shadowy buildings, numerous lights began to twinkle. Toward these the boys walked with bated breaths lest they be discovered.

"Let's sneak up behind that big one," Frank whispered, singling out a structure much larger than the rest.

It took them several moments to cover the remaining distance. At length they found themselves a few feet away from the place. They could hear the drone of many voices inside.

"There's a window," said Joe. "I think it's open."

He pointed at a small blotch in the wall. Stealing up to it they found that it was indeed open. Joe climbed up on his brother's shoulder to get a look at the room beyond. He dropped down a couple of minutes later.

"It's a mess hall," he said. "Filled with men. Must be a thousand of them! One fellow just announced a special meeting would be held there in an hour. Said the chief from New

York would speak and that everybody must attend.''

''While they're inside we can have the rest of the place to ourselves,'' whispered his brother jubilantly.

''In the meantime let's lie low in that shed over there,'' Joe proposed.

The boys scurried over the bare ground, peering furtively to right and left. Arriving at the door they stopped and strained eyes and ears.

''Give it a shove,'' urged Joe.

Gingerly Frank twisted the knob, expecting it to remain firm. To his delight it yielded, and the door swung open on a black interior. As he moved inside the lad stumbled over something.

''What is it?'' asked Joe in an excited whisper.

''I don't know. Feels like a heavy box,'' Frank replied, fumbling in the darkness. ''Jumping willigers, Joe, it's ammunition!''

''Really?''

''Yes. Whole box full of good-sized bullets. I'm holding one in my hand.''

Joe advanced to his brother's side, then struck out on his own. It was only a matter of seconds before he, too, tripped over a box. Like the other, it turned out to be filled with large caliber shells. A few moments' further investigation convinced the boys that the shack was a veritable ammunition dump.

''We'd better get out of here while we still

have a chance," Frank suggested. "Gee, they must be getting ready for a big war."

"They *are*—if they're really spies," Joe grunted. "Personally I think we ought to strike a match and blow the whole place to kingdom come."

"Not so fast. We've still a lot of evidence to get before we can really prove anything."

"I have an idea," proposed Frank. "Let's separate and meet here later. I'll try to get into the conference somehow. You look around and see what else you can find."

"Good. I may as well start now."

Squeezing his brother's hand Joe slipped away. For an hour he flitted about among the many buildings, taking great care to see that he was not discovered. At length he saw throngs moving in the direction of the mess hall. Flattening himself against the wall of a structure he waited until the last stragglers had disappeared.

"Now for some fast work," he said, smiling to himself. He stood for a moment wondering which building to enter first. "There's an official looking place," he decided at length.

Stealing up to the rear of an unlighted structure about five hundred yards from the eating place, the boy cautiously tried a door. To his delight it opened. Joe whipped out a pencil flashlight and followed the tiny beam into a large room filled with desks and typewriters.

For several moments he poked about among

stacks of correspondence, statistical charts and letters. From time to time he jotted down notes on a sheet of paper, then stuffed it into his pocket.

"I guess that will do for this place." He swung the beam of his light about for a last look. "Hello, there's an interesting looking door."

It bore a sign in a language unfamiliar to him. Joe touched the knob and the panel swung open. Aiming his flash, the boy discovered a stairway. At the bottom rays of light passed through the chinks of another door. Quickly he snapped off his switch.

There was not a sound from below. For a moment Joe wondered whether to take the chance of investigating or not. Finally he decided to do so. Cautiously he descended the stone steps.

At the bottom he saw that he was in a narrow passage, leading past a row of heavy doors. Through the crack of the one directly in front of him he could see feeble rays of light.

What to do now? Inside the room Joe thought he could hear the scratching of a pen. For a moment his impulse was to open the door. Then he realized how foolhardy such a move would be.

Trip! Trop! Trip! Trop! came the muffled echo of footfalls on the floor above. To Joe's dismay they rapidly came nearer, then the door through which he had just passed at the head of the staircase squeaked open.

"I must get out of here," thought the boy excitedly.

There was not an instant to lose. Desperately the Hardy lad leaped from where he was standing to the nearest panel past the lighted one. Making sure the room beyond was dark he gave the door a push. With a prayer of thanks he felt it yield. Then he snapped on his flashlight.

At the same instant the heavy footfalls came down the stairs. Apparently there were two people. Frantically Joe peered around for a place in which to conceal himself. Suddenly he saw a closet. Into this he squeezed himself just as two men marched into the room and switched on a bright light.

"Give me your coat, Henry. I'll hang it up for you," boomed a voice.

The hiding boy nearly fainted as he heard the man approaching but got behind some garments. The door swung open and two wet raincoats were hung up carelessly. Joe's heart had been pounding until he thought it would burst.

"Oh, look here," came one of the voices at that instant. "These specifications are—incorrect."

"Incorrect?" queried the second speaker.

"Anyhow, the tunnel is—finished," he heard the first man remark at length. "But that's nothing. Wait till I tell you about—our *next* job!"

"You have the—plans to show me?"

"Yes. But I think they are in—Room 18. Come with me."

The outer door opened and shut. The footsteps shuffled away. Heaving a mighty sigh of relief Joe waited a moment to be sure the men were not returning, then he crept from his hiding place. To his horror someone was just entering the room through another entrance. The boy stood rooted to the spot.

"Why, how do you do?" greeted a gentle voice. "You are a newcomer to our midst, are you not?"

Joe stared at the person before him. The man was elderly and his face seemed kindly. A shock of magnificent white hair tumbled over his brow like the spray of a waterfall. Joe opened his mouth but no words would come.

"What country are you from?" asked the old man, smiling pleasantly. "Come, do not be afraid to answer."

Joe still could say nothing. The stranger then began to speak again, but this time his language was not understood by the Hardy lad. Once or twice he recognized a familiar word in one tongue or another, but he could make no sense of what was being said.

Suddenly a bold idea flashed through the boy's excited brain. He waited for the speaker to pause, then looked him full in the face and asked:

"Are you by any chance Professor Morse, sir?"

CHAPTER XXIII

A NARROW ESCAPE

The white-haired old man smiled at Joe. "Why, yes, I am Professor Morse. Why do you ask?"

The boy was nonplussed. He had expected the missing teacher to be astounded at the question. Apparently this was not the Professor Morse who had disappeared.

The man's eyes were still upon Joe questioningly. "Why do you ask?" he repeated. "You seem surprised."

Swallowing his dismay the lad decided he had best explain. "I have been looking for a Professor Morse who once was on the faculty of Bixby University. The police all over the country have been looking for him ever since he disappeared mysteriously."

The gentleman had risen from his chair and stood staring at Joe wide-eyed. "What is that, young man? Did you say that Professor *Morse* —of Bixby University—*disappeared?*"

Joe nodded vigorously. "Yes, sir. Several years ago. I thought you might be he when you spoke so fluently a few minutes ago in all those tongues. Professor Morse was known as a language expert and——"

He gave a sudden start of alarm. Loud footsteps were approaching in the corridor outside their door.

"Why, what is the matter, young man?" asked the linguist, noting Joe's expression.

"Please, sir, I—I am not supposed to be here," the Hardy boy whispered hastily.

He peered around in desperation. Then, to his joy, Professor Morse winked a solemn gray eye and picked up a placard reading "Do Not Disturb." This he hung quickly over the outside of the door knob. Then he slammed the door. An instant later the footsteps came to a halt just outside. There was a muttered curse, then the sound moved on again.

The Professor chuckled. "I am always hanging that sign out. The men don't like it but they respect it, for they value my work."

He sat down in a chair and motioned Joe toward another. The boy's heart was pounding. Could this be the missing person he was looking for, after all?

"Now then, young man," the teacher began, "suppose you tell me why you are here and why, as you say, the whole country is looking for me."

Joe regarded the speaker in bewilderment mixed with joy at his discovery. "Why, Professor Morse, you—you have disappeared!"

"Disappeared?"

"Yes. You went on a vacation several years ago and—aud never came back. You left some important work unfinished and—and—" Too much at sea to continue Joe threw up his hands and stopped.

Professor Morse's brow was deeply furrowed. For a long time he stared gravely at the lad. Then slowly he began to speak.

"Young man, you have given me the greatest shock of my life. I had no intention of disappearing. While I was out here one summer, studying various Western dialects, I became acquainted with a man very much interested in root formations of language."

"What was his name?" asked Joe.

"Henry Bumper," came the startling reply.

Professor Morse went on to tell how he had revealed to this man his ability to make anyone speak in any dialect he might wish, just as an actor is required to do.

"Mr. Bumper offered me an interesting position at this place, teaching foreigners to speak like Yankees, Westerners, Southerners; in fact, like the natives in any particular section where these aliens intended to settle down and go into business."

"Bixby University never heard from you that you weren't coming back," said Joe.

The professor smiled. "I had an indefinite leave of absence, and I am not a person who ever writes letters."

Joe knew the elderly scholar was telling the truth and he disliked bringing to light what the man must be told. Yet time was precious. He tried, however, to lead up to the subject as gently as possible.

"Are there other professors here?" he asked. "And what else is taught?"

"There are no other university men," the elderly scholar replied. "I believe there are classes on business subjects. I never paid any attention. I was too busy teaching and writing up my reports."

"Professor Morse, didn't you eat with the men and go to their meetings?"

"No, no, I kept to myself," came the vigorous reply. "I had my meals alone with the head men and spent the rest of my time in my rooms. They are adjoining ones along this corridor; very pleasant, too, with windows overlooking a garden and——"

Joe felt he could wait no longer. This amiable, talkative man must be informed at once of the state of affairs.

"Professor Morse, this is a training camp for spies being taught to overthrow our government!" he said finally.

The listener all but leaped from his chair, white with indignation. "Young man, do you know what you are saying?" he demanded sternly.

Joe nodded calmly. "I do, Professor."

"Very well, let me hear what you have to tell!"

Starting with the Hardy boys' meeting with Professor Transor in the restaurant, Joe recounted in detail their subsequent experiences. When he had finished there were tears in the teacher's eyes.

"To think that I should have been duped so easily," he said sadly. Then he shook his magnificent head indignantly. "And to realize that I, of all people, should have elped in the education of plotters against the United States Government!"

Joe interrupted the silence that followed. "Professor Morse, will you leave the colony with my brother and me?"

"Will I? I should say I will. The sooner the better, young man."

"It probably won't be as easy as it sounds," Joe warned. "These people won't let you get away if they can help it."

"No, probably not," replied the man thoughtfully. "What have you to suggest?"

"We have a ladder ready. Can you scale the sapling fence tonight?"

"Tonight?"

"Yes, Professor."

"Then I must gather together some of my important papers. They will prove to be powerful evidence. I shall meet you outside in thirty minutes. But, goodness me, where? He chuckled. "1 am not used to escaping from places, young man. I do not know the art of it very well."

"We'll go to the shed near the south wall. Do you know where that is?"

"The shed? Oh, yes. I sometimes go for walks in that direction with Mr. Bumper. Very well. Now come here. . . ."

The kindly gentleman led Joe to a little-used door where the lad slipped directly outside.

"Now to find Frank," he whispered to himself. Looking toward the mess hall he had an inspiration. "The meeting's still in progress. Probably he'll be there."

He hurried through the darkness, taking a roundabout route that brought him to the rear window of the place, where he and his brother had stood before.

It was open. He could hear a fiery voice delivering a speech. Before he could comprehend what was being said a hand touched his elbow. Whirling around in sudden alarm he almost laughed aloud with relief.

"Sh," whispered Frank. He motioned Joe to follow him. When they were out of earshot the older lad stopped. "That's Trett, Joe! Boy, I heard him say enough to convict the whole mob and send them all to prison for life."

"That's not the half of it," his brother replied elatedly. Frank's eyes widened in surprise as Joe related the circumstances of his discovery of Professor Morse. "He'll be at the

shed in a few minutes. We'd better get started
while the going's good.''

Tingling with excitement the boys hastened
through the gloom and soon arrived at the old
shack. The elderly teacher was not yet there.

''Question is, how are we going to get away
even after we're ~ver the wall?'' Frank speculated. ''They'll miss the professor in an hour
or so and be out after him with a searching
party. Then they'll nab us, too.''

''I shouldn't be surprised,'' Joe admitted.
''I have an idea,'' he added, looking at his
watch. ''Frank, the *Flying Express* goes
through this region in a little while!''

''Think we can make it?''

''We'll *have* to. Here's hoping Professor
Morse can stand a fast hike. It's a good thing
it has stopped raining.''

''If we can get to the tracks in time, then
what?'' Frank asked.

''We'll flag the train.''

''Then we'll have to find a light of some sort.''

''Right. I think I remember seeing an old
lantern lying behind that ammunition shed,
Frank. Wait here and I'll get it.''

''Careful!'' the elder Hardy warned.

He watched with misgivings as Joe rushed off
through the gloom. As for his brother, he threw
all caution to the winds and made directly for
the distant building. After all, he reasoned,
the success of their whole venture depended on
that lantern.

Hearing footsteps on a gravel walk near by he stopped and held his breath. They passed. Joe hurried on again, hoping he would not lose his way. Suddenly his heart leaped. The storehouse was right in front of him. It was unlighted.

Stealthily the boy crept around behind and began fumbling in the grass. There was a dull *clank* as his fingers struck a metal object. With a whispered cry of triumph he raised the lantern.

"Suppose it's empty?" he mumbled.

As he swung the can, a faint swish sounded within. Grinning with delight Joe grabbed the lamp's handle and dashed back.

"That you, Joe?" came a whisper.

"Right. I found the lantern!"

Eagerly the boys examined their prize but decided against striking a match until later. Frank looked at his radium-dial watch.

"Where's your friend the professor? He's past due already."

"He'll be here any minute. Listen!"

A faint rustling sound in the misty dusk gradually merged into the crunch of footsteps. A moment later the scholarly man stepped up, his arms laden with brief cases and sheafs of papers. Joe introduced his brother.

"Well, boys," said Professor Morse briskly, "let's be going. Where is your ladder?"

If the boys had any misgivings about the venerable person's ability to scale a wall on a vine ladder they were agreeably surprised. The old man scooted over the fence with remarkable speed. Frank and Joe followed quickly, heaving sighs of relief as they dropped safely on the other side.

"Now where?" queried Professor Morse. "As a scholar I like to have specific plans awaiting me at all times. Otherwise I find it impossible to make decisions."

The brothers laughed at their genial friend's peppery humor. Then they settled down to the grim task at hand. With the pencil flashlight they discovered the first bugle trail mark and soon were on their way. Frank decided it would be safe to light the lantern now.

"It won't work," he said in dismay, as match after match spluttered out over the wick.

"Never mind, we'll try when we get to the tracks. We'd better not waste time here."

It was rough going. Frank glanced at his watch frequently with a worried frown. At intervals the boys paused to listen for sounds of possible pursuit.

"If my ears don't deceive me I hear the baying of hounds," said Professor Morse as they neared the end of the wooded trail.

In desperation the three doubled their speed. At length, with the elderly man ready to drop from sheer exhaustion, they reached the open field. Soon they found themselves alongside the tracks.

"No train," Joe grunted.

"If I'm not mistaken, there it comes."

A bright beam of light had just appeared far down the ties. Slowly it grew larger, and the boys could hear the distant thunder of a powerful engine.

"Quick! More matches," Joe exclaimed tensely as he stooped over the lantern.

Frank emptied his pockets of half a dozen.

"Confound that wind," the younger boy exploded as the third flame went out.

The roar of the train grew steadily louder, and the beam of its headlight glistened on the steel rails beside them.

"There! It's lighted," Frank suddenly exclaimed.

The words were scarcely out of his mouth when the feeble splutter died out.

"More matches," Joe gasped.

"Here are two," said Frank dolefully. "They're the last I have."

Excitedly Joe, Frank and the professor grouped themselves around the lamp in a desperate attempt to cut off the breeze. Joe struck his last match. With shouts of triumph they watched the wick flare up. There was not an instant to lose, for the express was bearing down on them swiftly.

"Stay here," Joe gasped. "I'll run down the track as far as I can."

A hundred yards distant the boy stopped. Then, as the train roared toward him, he waved the lantern frantically.

CHAPTER XXIV

THE SPY CAMP

WITH a grinding screech the train lurched to a stop some distance beyond them. Whooping with joy the boys fairly dragged Professor Morse with them in their haste to get aboard. Before they could reach the last car they saw the conductor approaching, pointing a large flashlight in their direction.

"What's the meaning of this?" the official demanded, peering at their faces. "Is somebody hurt?"

"We're sorry to have troubled you, sir," Frank replied breathlessly, "but we must get to Saddler immediately. We——"

"You stopped this train so's you could get a ride to Saddler?" thundered the man. "Don't you know you might have injured the passengers making us stop suddenly? I'll have the law on you!"

Several other railroad employees got off the train and hurried over.

"Can you beat that?" snarled the first conductor. "These young whippersnappers and this man stopped us so's they could get a ride!"

"Take 'em aboard," broke in an authoritative voice, apparently coming from one of the other trainmen. "Maybe they had somethin' to do with yesterday's wreck. We'll take 'em to Saddler, all right—to the cooler they have there. It's got nice bars on it."

Before the boys could say another word they were marched into the last car, with Professor Morse behind them.

"Sit down here," ordered the chief conductor, pointing to three vacant seats. "Charley, stay with 'em and see they remain right here."

A brakeman detached himself from the group and sat alongside the professor, while Frank and Joe were permitted to sit together. Finally, after what seemed an eternity to the impatient brothers, the engine jerked to a stop.

"You'll have to wait here till we get you an escort," said their guard sarcastically. A few moments later he motioned to them. "All right, step lively."

With Professor Morse behind them Frank and Joe stepped off the train. Suddenly Frank gave a start and dug his elbow into his brother's side.

"Don't I see somebody we know?"

"Howling tomcats, Frank, it's that door-lock fixer! What's he doing around here?" Joe stared in astonishment.

"We'll have to catch him later," Joe whispered, as the man disappeared in a waiting sedan.

One spy more or less did not matter to the

boys at this moment. Their main problem now was to communicate with their father as soon as possible.

"These three flagged us without just cause," announced the conductor to the station agent. "You got a deputy around here to arrest 'em?"

The man gave a low whistle and a fellow in uniform stepped forward.

"Some trouble?" he asked.

When the difficulty was explained, he took the prisoners in his car to the sheriff's office. Secretly this was just what the boys wanted.

"You flagged the *Flying Express* without just cause?" said Sheriff Homan when told the circumstances.

"We flagged the train, sir, but not without just cause," replied Frank coolly.

He reached into his pocket and deposited his card of identification before the man.

"Hm," said the latter. "Fenton Hardy's son, are you? We know yore father's reputation right well."

"Please, sir, may I have a word with you in private?" the boy asked.

The sheriff stood up. "You certainly may, young man, if you're Detective Hardy's boy. Come this way."

When Frank and the official were closeted in an inner room, part of the story came out. Then the telephone wires began to hum. After a while the Hardy youth burst into the outer room, bristling with news.

"Mother says Dad's in Beegle, Joe! He's at the Scudder House. He's using the name of Hazen."

"I'll phone him," offered the younger lad excitedly. In a few minutes he reported, "I got him, Frank! He'll be here early in the morning. Fast as he can make it."

After a meal at a restaurant, which stayed open late, the boys and the professor sought a hotel and engaged rooms. The man retired at once in his own room, while the brothers sat up late talking things over. Finally, exhausted after their strenuous experiences, they fell asleep.

A loud pounding at their door awakened them in the dimness of early morning. Groggy from heavy sleep, Joe tumbled out of bed and hesitantly pulled it open.

"Dad!" he cried joyously.

"It's about time you boys were up," the famous detective said heartily.

He marched in, followed by none other than Kelly with his customary cigar. "Howdy, everybody," the fat man said breezily. He went over and pulled the covers off Frank. "Get up, lazybones! It's five o'clock!"

At once the group settled down to discuss the serious business at hand.

"First," said Mr. Hardy, "I want to hear in detail everything you have experienced since I last saw you."

The brothers took turns relating what had

happened. At intervals their father nodded his approval. When they had completed their account it was evident from the detective's expression that Mr. Hardy was highly pleased.

"Very good work, boys," he said enthusiastically. "Now, I have some of my agents ready outside. I shall have one group go to the ranch house for your friend Pete Rangle, the fake rancher. Another group I shall dispatch to various places around the town of Beegle. I suspect the police and half the town of being in league with the spies."

Frank looked up in surprise. "Golly, I *thought* they acted queer when we asked them to get Kelly's car."

"The third band of agents will accompany us to the camp site. Are you ready?"

"*Are we!*" exclaimed both youths in a single breath.

The professor was awakened and told of the plan. One man was left to guard him, as Mr. Hardy feared for the old man's life, should the spies learn his whereabouts.

Frank winked at Joe as the brothers went outside and found a line of cars in front of the hotel. "Dad's efficiency, as usual," he laughed. "I'll bet he has nearly every federal agent in the country here!"

Several moments passed while Mr. Hardy went to each of the autos in turn and gave his orders. At last he returned to the leading one in which there was only a driver.

"Hop in, boys," he said breezily.

Following his directions they drove directly to the station. To the lads' amazement a train consisting of an engine and several empty coaches was awaiting them. In it were many armed men.

"All aboard," said Fenton Hardy briskly. "We'll ride to that hidden camp."

"Our private *Flying Express*," Joe laughed in delight. He looked at his father admiringly. "Dad, you think of *everything*, don't you?"

After a quick run the train came to a stop, at Frank's suggestion, near the point where the boys had waved the lantern the night before.

"This is as close as we can get?" Mr. Hardy asked his son.

At the latter's nod he hustled the men out and across the field toward the woods. There, led by the boys, they picked out a certain trail and after a time reached the high sapling fence.

"We used a vine ladder here, Dad," Frank remarked.

"Good work," said the detective. "Fortunately we have plenty of rope. Crosby!"

One of the agents stepped up. "Yes, sir."

"Get out the rope and fix something up in a hurry. We must get inside at once."

Several of the men huddled together talking while the others poked curiously at the high fence. A few moments later Crosby stepped up to Mr. Hardy.

"We're ready, sir."

"All right, throw them over."

Counterbalanced with sharp steel hooks half a dozen strands of hemp snaked out through the air and caught onto the top of the fence. Fenton Hardy nodded, and the agents clambered over the barricade. The detective and his sons followed.

No one was in sight when they gathered together on the other side. Smoke could be seen drifting from the chimney of one of the distant buildings, but otherwise there was no sign of activity.

"Keep your eyes open and your guns cocked, men," rapped out Mr. Hardy. "They'll be a tough bunch to handle when they see us."

Like an invading army the group marched boldly forward while Frank and Joe followed with wildly beating pulses. Then Mr. Hardy ordered a halt.

"Jackson, take three of the men and circle around to the left. Crosby, take three men and do the same on the right. The rest of us will continue straight ahead."

Mr. Hardy's band moved ahead toward a large structure several hundred yards away. There was still no sign of the inhabitants of the community.

"Looks like they're all takin' a vacation," grunted Kelly, panting with exertion. "Don't see a blasted critter no place."

Frank and Joe themselves thought it strange that they had not been challenged, but said nothing. When they reached the mess hall, and still had seen no spies, their spirits sank.

Joe touched his father's arm. "There's the building where I found Professor Morse, Dad. I think it's the main one. Let's go in there."

At an affirmative nod the younger Hardy led the detectives up the front steps. One of the men shoved at the door with the butt of his gun. It swung open slowly, revealing a large room—utterly bare. Frank and Joe gaped at the scene in dismay.

All right, men, scatter around the whole place and report to me here in ten minutes," ordered Mr. Hardy. Then he looked at his crestfallen sons. "Don't worry, boys, it's not your fault. Besides, we haven't investigated everything yet."

Sick at heart, Frank and Joe sat down on the steps with their father. So the spies had escaped! One by one the agents returned, each with the same dismal report. The entire camp was strangely deserted.

CHAPTER XXV

CLOSING THE CASE

JOE took his brother aside from the milling group. "There's one chance left, Frank, even if it's a small one."

"Doesn't matter how small it is if it works. What is it?"

"When I was down in the basement of this place, hiding in a closet, I heard a man talking about a tunnel they'd just finished. Do you suppose——"

"By golly, they *might* be hiding in one," Frank exclaimed in a low voice. "I don't see how they could have cleared out so fast otherwise."

"I'll tell Dad."

Joe hurried over to where Mr. Hardy was conversing grimly with several of the government men. Joe repeated what he had told Frank.

"There's no harm looking for one," said the detective. "Boys, come here a minute." The other agents swarmed around him expectantly. "I want every square inch of this camp and every building in it searched for a possible secret underground passage or room. Find that tunnel if there's one to be found."

Eager for something to do the men dispersed in all directions. Frank and Joe decided to do some scouting on their own and selected the basement where Joe had met Professor Morse. For more than an hour they poked about with their flashlights, pounding the metal work, thumping panels, and scrutinizing floors and ceilings.

"Well, there's only one thing left to look at and that's the trap door or whatever it is up there on that wall," Frank commented at length.

"Shucks, nobody could get through that, it's too small," Joe decided. For a moment they stared at the spot, which was higher than they could reach.

"I've a hunch we'd better investigate it, Joe," said Frank. "Let's find something to stand on."

So thoroughly had the camp and its buildings been vacated that it was some time before they could find anything whatever to use as a support. Finally Joe turned up with an old crate.

"Here," he said. "Try this."

By standing on tiptoe on top the box Frank could just reach the trap door. He gave it a thump. A hollow echo rolled away. Suddenly the lad uttered an exclamation.

"What's the matter?" Joe called.

"Get Dad and his men quick! This trap door is only part of the *real* opening. I can see the seams running right through the stone."

Excitedly Joe rushed upstairs. Five minutes

later he was back with Mr. Hardy and a group of the agents. Frank looked down from his perch and described what he had found.

"Jackson," called the detective, "have you that pocket drill with you?"

"Yes, Mr. Hardy."

The man pulled something bulky from his pocket. Another agent stepped alongside and fished two large batteries from beneath his coat. Two minutes later a powerful drill had been set up and connected to the current.

Jackson walked up to the wall beneath the trap door, his instrument poised. There was a sudden *whir*, then a prolonged splintering sound. Bits of plaster flew in all directions. Then came a loud *crunch* and the tool plunged through.

"Good work, Jackson," Mr. Hardy commended. "Keep it up."

For quarter of an hour the scouts manned the probe by turns. Frank and Joe watched with growing satisfaction as it became more evident with each departing lump of debris that a secret passage lay beyond.

"All right, that's enough," said Mr. Hardy at length. "Somebody stick a light in there."

The boys were joyous as a beam penetrated the blackness and revealed a large opening, the end of which they could not see.

"Williams, you and Jones take your guns and go in there," ordered the detective. "See what you find."

With bated breaths Frank and Joe waited until the agents returned. In disappointment they listened to the report that the tunnel ended not far away and was empty.

"No, it's not empty," snapped Fenton Hardy. "There's air in it, isn't there?"

Williams looked at the detective with a crestfallen expression. "Y-yes, sir, there's air, sir —but no people."

Mr. Hardy was standing alert with one hand poised upward. His men regarded him questioningly. The detective nodded toward Frank and Joe.

"Come over here, boys." Completely mystified the brothers advanced to their father's side. "Hold up your hands—like this," Mr. Hardy ordered. "Do you notice anything?"

"Yes," Frank exclaimed in a tense whisper. "I can feel a current of air."

"So can I, Dad," Joe burst out. "By golly, that must mean——!"

He stopped and regarded his father searchingly. Fenton Hardy smiled grimly.

"Exactly, Joe. It must mean that there's another opening to this tunnel besides the main entrance here."

"But where could that be, sir?" Williams queried with a puzzled look while a buzz of skeptical comment rose from the other agents.

"That's for us to find out," snapped Mr. Hardy.

Deliberately he seized a light from one of the

men and raised himself into the passage. Frank
and Joe followed eagerly. Without a word the
detective paced back and forth, thumping the
walls. Then he pointed the flash upward to
look at the ceiling. Suddenly he stopped as a
mass of tiny holes was revealed. Taking out a
penknife he began scraping. Frank and Joe,
watching intently, suddenly saw the seams of a
trap door gradually assume outline before
them.

"Come in here, men," Mr. Hardy suddenly
ordered. The agents filed forward. "Smith,
pry out this grate. You have a chisel with you,
haven't you?" He turned toward the other
scouts. "Have your guns ready, men."

There was a sudden clang as the metal work
crashed to the floor, and a chorus of exclama-
tions rose up from the onlookers.

"Quiet!" commanded the detective. "Listen!"

The muffled murmur of many voices was distinctly audible somewhere above them. Frank's
heart leaped in anticipation.

"All right, men, swing yourselves up there
and be ready for trouble," said his father.

The Hardy boys begged to be allowed to follow the others up through the trap door, but
their parent shook his head. "Not yet," he
said.

The words were hardly out of his mouth when
there was a blast of gunfire from above, then
another and a third, followed by a chorus of

yells. Just as abruptly, all became quiet. A moment later Williams poked his head through the trap door.

"All right, Mr. Hardy, we got 'em covered."

"Good." The detective turned to his sons. "Go ahead up, boys."

Eagerly the brothers pulled themselves through the aperture into what appeared to be another long passage similar to the one below.

"Follow me," said Williams.

They marched behind the agent for several moments. Suddenly, turning a bend in the damp corridor, they found themselves blinking in a strong light, in a huge vaulted room literally jammed with men cowering in front of the poised guns.

Mr. Hardy stepped up behind his sons. "Just what I thought," he said. "Frank, Joe, did you notice that steep rise in the ground outside? Well, we're inside the hill right now."

The agents quickly lined the men up and snapped handcuffs on each in turn. As the manacled spies were marched out in single file the lads from Bayport recognized the locksmith who followed Trett, and each of the others whom they had discovered on the *Flying Express*.

"See that runt of a fellow there?" Mr. Hardy said in a low voice. The boys nodded as a short, slender man passed by. "Your Aunt Gertrude gets the credit for catching him."

Joe looked at his father questioningly. The

detective was chuckling. "Remember the phone conversation I was having with you, Frank, when I stopped all of a sudden?"

"That was when Aunt Gertrude whacked one of your clients over the head with—" Joe stopped with his mouth wide open in astonishment. "Was *that* the man, Dad?"

Mr. Hardy nodded vigorously. "He was, Joe. That was my one-time client, Andrew Court. I didn't find out until later that he was a member of this gang. In the meantime Aunt Gertrude should be praised for having kept him from hearing what I might have said to Frank over the phone about our plans."

Both boys laughed, and Joe said, "Good old Auntie. She'll be a detective yet, Frank!"

"I'll say so. You know, Joe, I think Aunt Gertrude deserves a reward for that, don't you?"

"I certainly do, and I know what it ought to be. Let's treat her to a real trip West on——"

"On the *Flying Express!*"

Directed by Fenton Hardy, the federal agents conducted their captives to a makeshift headquarters back in Saddler. For several days the detective and his sons questioned the men. Professor Morse readily agreed to take part in the proceedings and identified the prisoners as men whom he had taught to speak correct English.

One by one, under Mr. Hardy's gruelling questions, the spies confessed to their part in the huge ring. Trett and Pete Rangle, together with the special agents whom Frank and Joe had trailed on the *Flying Express*, were particularly stubborn but even they broke down and confessed.

"If it had not been for those—young gentlemen—we should not have been—exposed," Waxen said bitterly, looking at Frank and Joe with eyes full of hate. "Some day their—smartness—will get them in—serious trouble."

The boys smiled, for they never let threats deter them. They would be ready for their next case, no matter how dangerous—and dangerous "The Clue in the Broken Blade" was to be.

But that was in the future. Now they were about to leave for home with their father and Professor Morse.

"To think that I was responsible for teaching those spies the English language," the scholarly man moaned as they sped over the prairie in a luxurious train. "I—I cannot believe it! I must have been completely mad to have been fooled so easily. No one will want me again for any work."

"You weren't fooled easily, Professor Morse," Mr. Hardy remarked. "Those men are clever."

"The government is waiting for you to get back to finish your translations of those ancient chemical formulas," Frank added.

Fenton Hardy nodded. "You will be very welcome in Washington, Professor."

By the time the boys reached Bayport the whole country was ringing with the exciting news of the break-up of the spy camp and the finding of Professor Morse. At the station the Hardys received a thunderous welcome.

The days that followed brought hosts of telegrams, some congratulating them and others telling of interesting episodes at Beegle. It had been proved that the hotel fire had been caused by one of the spies. Since the owner would not come to terms with men at the camp, orders had come to burn down his place.

Another message said members of the subversive group had been experimenting on plans to get supplies more easily to the hidden storehouse. Unwittingly they had run a freight train onto the wrong track and caused the disastrous wreck of the great giant of the rails.

Later Frank and Joe were called as witnesses at the trial of the spies. Then one day, less than a week after everything was cleared up, the brothers went to watch the great *Flying Express* as it roared through Bayport. Aboard the most luxurious sleeper, surrounded by boxes of candy and dressed in all her finery, sat none other than Aunt Gertrude.

"Dear me," she was saying to herself, "Frank and Joe really aren't such annoying boys after all!"

THE END